Tales of the S.S. No-Where

By Asa Henry

Copyright notice

Copyright © 2022 by Asa James Henry.

All rights reserved. No part of this book may be reproduced in any form or by any electronic or mechanical means, including information storage and retrieval systems, without permission in writing from the publisher, except by a reviewer who may quote brief passages in a review.

First U.K Edition

Contest Page

Chapter One .... The Cooper has landed

Chapter Two .... Meeting the Crew

Chapter Three .... Game of cards?

Chapter Four .... Can I play Cards?

Chapter Four .... Part two

Chapter Five .... O Captain my Captain

Chapter Six .... Worrying Times

Chapter Seven .... The Spy is Found

Chapter Eight .... Pirates!!

Chapter Nine .... Space Pirates?

Chapter Ten .... New Friends

Chapter Eleven................ The Escape Plan

Chapter Twelve................ Accidents Happen in Space

Chapter Thirteen .... Panda's Friend

Chapter One

The Cooper has Landed

Cooper takes a look out of the window of the jump shuttle to see the new ship he is going to be calling home for the rest of his military life. Floating in space he could see the S.S. No-Where. After a very poor showing at the academy, he was just happy to pass and be assigned to a ship, even if it was with the lowest score in the history of the academy, he passed! That in itself was an impossibility because the Fleet academy has been running for over 3000 years. The rules of the Fleet Academy itself were changed so he could pass with such a low score. Normally with such a case like this where a family was buying the passing grade for a family member a test would be fixed or extra work grade added. His case was the highest profile person to go through the academy in the past 1000 years so it was very hard to use the normal ways of cheating the system. Cooper himself was not the high-profile person but his family. He hated this. Always asking the same questions over and over he was so happy to be out where none would know him. All of that was now in the past he could start his new life make new friends that didn't know him that didn't know his family name.

Cooper looks back into the jump shuttle with a big smile on his face.

"What's with the stupid smile?" a voice said.

Looking over he could see a man with black hair and a very serious look on his face or was it a look of stress?

"Hi" Cooper said.

The man answered sharply "You didn't answer my question but said hi. Did you understand the question?" The tone was of deep sarcasm and the man didn't make eye contact with cooper.

"O" Cooper said "I thought it was a question to break the ice, my name is Cooper what's yours"

"What are you 12? And I can read" The sarcastic voice says back pointing at his own name tag. "It's like the military put little name tags and ranks on people so without knowing someone you can know them just by looking at them"

"o" Cooper said again feeling the happy smile leave him" Hi office Feet please, to meet you"

"It's Fett you idiot, you can't read and its 1st lieutenant it shows you on my arm!" The lieutenant yelled. "My god you are a second lieutenant you should know what rank your boss is!"

Coopers smile now had completely gone. The happy feeling of starting a new life and putting his past problems from the academy had gone. This Fett guy, his new boss just killed that happy puppy feeling he had. Not less than 10 seconds ago he felt like a new puppy that found the out-side world for the first time and everything was a new smell and something amazing to play with. All taken away with a tone of voice to him which was too familiar. The tone was you are a loser shut up before I kill you. Well, that's how it felt. Now the puppy spirit had its nose hit for getting out of the house and thrown back into its cage with a dry water bowl no blanket no food just the metal cage floor. This feeling would make him go into survival mode which he knew too well.

"I apologies senior officer Fett" Cooper said trying to put on his best military voice. "I hope we didn't get off on the wrong foot" Thinking in his head, you should have said feet!

"I don't understand why you are smiling so much about being sent to this ship, you understand what this ship is right? It's called the no-where for a reason." Fett bringing the conversation back to the reason he asked the question about him smiling in the first place. Fett however was wrong about the ship being called the No-Where because it means your career was going nowhere. That is just a coincidence the name of the ship matches the rest of your career path, life and everything that's going to happen to you. You are going nowhere.

The No-Where is a battle cruiser class ship which they don't make anymore. The fleet has over 33,000 active ships flying about with over half fighting in the war. The No-Where is not going to war or any place noteworthy. It's a dumping ground for anything the military doesn't want needs to forget or hide. No one wants to go to this ship you are sent kicking and screaming so the question in the back of Fett's mind wouldn't go away. Why was that kid smiling about coming on this ship?

"I was smiling about being back in space, SIR!" Cooper said to the officer. It was a total lie which

Cooper never used to feel comfortable doing but after being in the Fleet Academy it seemed to be coming second nature to him.

"Not much of a space guy myself Cooper" Fett said.

"I love it" Cooper replied.

"Well, I best start loving it to, as I am going to be in it for a long time" Fett said with a sad tone. "What did you do Cooper to get put on this hell hole?"

"I didn't Sir "Cooper chirped back.

"Everyone has done something terrible Cooper, its why people get sent to this ship. It's a dump for anything the fleet doesn't want, everyone knows that." Fett added still in the sad tone. Cooper didn't know which tone he liked more the sarcastic tone or the sad one. The sarcastic one made Cooper feel stupid but the sad tone made him feel sorry for his new commanding office and he didn't want to feel sad for this man. Coopers brain then turned back on to the conversation.

"I did get the lowest score in fleet academy history" Cooper answered. He felt that he should tell him. Fett could look up his record on the ship anyway so he had no point to lie.

"Yep, that will do it" Fett Answered.

This was not the normal response to him saying this. It was normally followed by laughing that lasted about 2 mins then they never talked to him again. This was a shock so Cooper added.

"They changed the rules the day after so no one again could get a score as low as mine and be in the fleet, then I was sent here"

"Yep, they'll do that" Fett mumbled.

"Do what?" Cooper asked.

"Change the rules when they don't like something" Feet answered.

Cooper didn't want to say anything stupid so he stopped himself. A skill he picked up from many years of saying something stupid or showing his basic level of understanding was not there. As he was sitting with a stupid smile slowly coming back to his face an idea happened. Well, it didn't happen to was more like two planets moving or the death of a sun. Very slow. So slow and painful it took the smile off his face and now Cooper looked like he was in real pain.

Office Fett asked "Cooper are you ok? You look like you are in real pain!"

"No Sir" Cooper replied "I am fine just thinking about stuff"

Office Fett put one hand over his face to hide the look on it. It was clear something had to be done about this Cooper. Fett had never seen someone look like they were in so much pain trying to have a simple thought before. This was hurting him. He didn't think people did this in real life. Did people like this live in the universe, are they having kids? It did make the war make more sense if the rest of the universe was like this, he had some thinking to do later. Right now, something had to be done about this Cooper. Office Fett could not have someone like this under his control with less brain power than a house cat. How stupid was this kid? He did get the lowest score in the history of the fleet! All Fett was thinking about was the 1000's of ways this idiot was going to get him killed. Then a though came into his head, would he have to dress him in the morning? What about meals did he know how to feed himself? Back over in the vast waste land that was Coopers brain it seems he had worked out that Officer Fett was talking about himself not Cooper all this time. What Had Office Fett done to get sent to the No-Where? Cooper starting working on a plan about how to ask his new Commanding Officer without making him mad or sound stupid. I know, he said to himself. Make a joke. He was good at jokes everyone around him was always laughing at the things he said. Now should he use the one about who's mum did he sleep with? Yes, that's the one. Maybe he should change the mum to daughter? That would be safer to a commanding Officer. Cooper smiled proud of himself, not only did he work out why Office Fett was upset but worked out a joke they both would laugh about. So here goes Cooper told himself.

"So, Office Fett who did you sleep with, the Lord Grand Admirals daughter or something?" Cooper said with a big smile on his face waiting for the laugh as there is no way this can or could happen.

Fett's face changed to a scowl with sarcasm if you could have such a face then answered the young stupid Office.

"Yes, yes I did everyone knows this!" He yelled. "It's been on the news for 3 months. They tried to jail me. The enemy use it as propaganda!" He yelled some more. "How to you not know this!"

With this answer Cooper's brain broke. Well stopped working completely. He had to remind himself to breath and then without thinking (Shock) said.

"Well, if they wanted to put you in jail maybe you shouldn't have tried to rape her!" Cooper found himself yell back at the same level Office Feet which was a shock again but now he was breathing again so that was good.

"I didn't rape her!" Office screamed at him with his fingers making a fist on his right hand. "We have been in love from when we were kids!!"

Cooper's answer was so stupid that Office Fett found himself not breathing because of the stupid. O, know was the stupid catching? Could he die from this? He had to get away from this man because Cooper could get Fett killed or worse Fett killed Cooper out of rage. Cooper answered.

"kids? You shouldn't have sex with kids you should go to jail for that."

The only answer Office Fett could get back was

"She is the same age as me she is not a kid now!" Thinking to himself. Does it matter what I say to this kid? What's the point, he doesn't understand anything? A complex situation like this was going to go way over his head opening a door is past his pay grade. Everyone else could see it's about the class of his family and a political stich up because her Father was Lord Admiral Miku. His daughter could not marry someone like me the Admiral would never have it Fett repeated to himself. Just as he was about to yell a barge of insults at the kid that could possibly make the kid cry or maybe kill himself and he was good with both a buzzer sounded. The jump shuttles pilot came over the speakers informing them they had landed on the No-Where. Finally, time to get out of this conversation. Fett looked up to see a happy Cooper spring up off the flight chair to be slammed back down because he hadn't unlocked the 5-pointed harness holding him down. Round two of Cooper V the chair was a win for Cooper as he hit the button to release the harness thinking to himself "I am good at hitting Buttons "and with that jumped up running to the door. He hit the button to open the door. Well, he hit a button "I am good at hitting buttons" went off in his head again. It was a big red emergency lock down button. The cabin turned red buzzing happened and 1st Lieutenant Dan Fett looked like he was about to kill Cooper.

Chapter Two

Meeting the Crew

On the outside of the jump shuttle was ensign Chris. He seemed very quick to put in the override code turning off the emergency shut down. The door opened and the two new crew members stepped onto the Flight deck of their new home for the first time. As a battle cruiser the S.S. No-Where had not just a Fight deck to bring ships on but carried a full fighter squadron onboard. A full fighter squadron would be 12 ships the No-Where had only 3 with two that worked, sometimes. It could hold 2 full squadrons with space to spare. A battle cruiser was the Second largest ship in the fleet after a carrier. The Battle Cruiser was built not as a battle ship or a carrier but something in the middle. Something that could hold fighters and use them to kill a battle ship from a far or get right next to a carrier and blow it away with its deck guns. They stopped making battle cruisers years ago. So long ago in fact that the people that make up history can't say for sure. They do know it's around the time they worked out sending 400 carriers with 600 supporting ships with more than half being full battle ships and was the way to fight a war not this 1v1 ship combat ideas of the past. Just build more ships was the cry from the people in charge so they did. Now the Fleets all over the universe are so large in truth no one has a clue of the true number flying about but it's well over 33,000. Which is not a lot when you start to understand the size and true emptiness of space. Numbers wins. Ship building turned away from 1v1 model moving to the, 1000 v I will bring 1000 more ships if the first 1000 doesn't win and destroy you. This seems to be the best way in which to fight a war in space. Space was a different place to fight sometimes the hard part was just finding the enemy most of the time.

It was like trying to find the reason in Cooper's head why it was ok to hit the emergency lock down button. 1st Lieutenant Dan Fett had to ask him. No more than that, he needed to know how stupid this kid was so he could plot to have him as far as he could from himself to lower the risk of Cooper killing Office Fett out of total stupidity.

"Why did you hit the emergency lock down Cooper!" Office Fett said with a very loud and firm tone.

"It's ok." ensign Chris replies "Happens all the time here on the No-Where, seems like people think if they lock themselves in the shuttle, they don't to set foot here and by magic go back. That's why they send me. I know the code to every shuttle I have done this so many times." Chris was cut off speaking when beeping from the security monitor went off as Cooper walked past it. "Let me take a look at you" Chris said to Cooper. "It's normally the side arm that sets this thing off. The software is so old the newer guns set it off."

Fett answered "It didn't set mine off."

"That's why I said normally, Sir." With a great deal of sarcasm. Fett almost forgot not everyone was as Stupid as Cooper giving Chris a smile back letting Chris know that he got him with that one.

"Where is your side arm?" Chris then asked Cooper. Checking to see if that was the item that set the machine off.

Cooper was thinking. You could tell because his

eyes were off to one side and looking up at the same time with the look of, he was about to fart. "It's at the academy I think." Cooper slowly said.

 This being the first time Chris has seen the new level of stupidity Cooper was infecting the Galaxy with made his jaw drop. He stopped with his mouth open eyes wide staring at Cooper.

"You don't know where your side fire arm is?" Chris said. "Your gun. "Chris was talking in hope that Cooper would cut him off. Cooper did speak not making sense about anything thing just like normal.

"They didn't let me have guns or knives at the academy." He said. Office Fett started to laugh but stopped himself making a noise out of his nose. Leaned against the wall with a big smile on his face looking at the ensign and spoke. "It's for the best he doesn't have a weapon." Giving ensign Chris a knowing nod as if to say drop it. This talk could go on for hour if he didn't Fett was thinking. If this Cooper talks more maybe the stupid infecting Cooper would infect ensign Chris.   With that they all went to the ships transport system to see the captain.

      The doors to the ships transport system opened and before them was the ships bridge.

Captain Cheese was easy to spot sitting in a chair in the middle of the bridge looking at a view screen. Ships didn't have windows but view screens. It's more like ships in space can't have windows. With no windows what ships have is a muti-sensor system that plays onto screens to give the illusion of having windows. It's a very simple system of camera's playing to the screen on the other side of where the camera is mounted. Without windows its was found people felt sad much faster without the ability to look out at something so this system was made.

   Off to the far left was one more Officer. He was on the Navigation station and didn't look up at them even when ensign Chris started to talk. "Captain Cheese Sirrrrrrr" The ensign shouted. He shouted comically loud will his eyes closed tightly. Sounding like a drill instructor from the academy. A slight snigger from the Nav office could be heard but he still didn't look up.

   The Captain replied "Yes ensign"

"The two new Officers to replace the deaths of "when the ensign said deaths of, the Captain jumped in to cut off the last part of his sentence.

"Thank you, ensign, take your post." Captain Cheese said. With that the ensign moved over to the communication post and started to look busy. 1st Lieutenant Dan Fett's eyes could not get any wider after hearing the whole replace dead people thing. Cooper could kill him at any time by hitting a button on something and now his new job he is taking on could kill him as well. How was he ever going to get back to the love of his life. The captain snapped him out of the day dream with the words he was beginning to hate.

"So, the Lord Admiral Daughter then." His new captain said. He was clearly referring to the reason he was reassigned to the nowhere.

"It would seem to be so" Fett replied.

"Well welcome to the nowhere" the captain said back with a half-smile. "It's not as bad as everyone makes out. It's a very nice ship."

"I am sure the ship is fine, it's about getting off her, Sir." Office Fett said as fast as he could so the captain wouldn't cut him off. Would he ever stop thinking about trying to get back to his Catherine? Everything he did was to try to achieve that goal.

"I have had a very long talk with Lord Admiral Miku and it seems this is going to be your home for a very long time." Captain Cheese replied. Office Fett gave a knowing shrug and a funny little head nod showing he totally understood what the captain was saying.

"So, this quiet one must be Cooper then." The Captain had moved targets and his eyes switched over to Cooper. Office Fett folded his arms took a step back and smiled. It was like he could tell a show was about to start and couldn't wait to watch.

"Sir yes Sir I came on the shuttle with Office feet sir." Cooper said loud and proud.

"With Office Feet you say" The captain looking at the 1st Lieutenant raising his eyebrows when saying this. Looking for his new 1st Office to give him an answer.

"The boy can't read" Office Fett replied pointing at his name tag in hopes the captain would drop it.

"Is this true son?" The captain asked.

"I have some problems." Cooper answered.

"Well you are the 1st Lieutenants right hand man on MY bridge, if reading is a problem this might not be the place for you." The captain Barked at Cooper. In the back of Office Fett's mind getting Cooper away from him was top of his list of stupid crap that was going to kill him so he was happy to hear the captain's words. Just then the Nav Office said.

"Captain"

To get the captain to check something he had sent him.

"Thanks Office Spu" looking back at Cooper the captain's mood seemed to change after reading what he was sent. With a big smile he said to Cooper

"It's ok we have a place for you so you can take your time getting up to speed on everything. "Cooper looked happy but it was clear to anyone who talked to Cooper he didn't have a clue what was going on. "Ensign Chris please take Cooper to his new post; we will get 1st Lieutenant Feet a more suitable assistant"

"Yes sir." the ensign replied with a big smile on his face looking at 1st Lieutenant Dan Fett who just missed the captain calling him Office Feet. He walked over to Cooper and said "let's go then." Cooper looked at him like he didn't know what to do. "It's ok." ensign Chris tried to reassure Cooper with a smile and it worked. They both stepped into the ships transport system and the door closed. Office feet was working on his death list. Cooper was gone now why did the old first Officer die? Easy lets asked the captain.

"Captain Cheese." he asked

"Yes first Officer." the Captain replied

"How did your old first Officer die? You said I was here to replace him?"

"We can save that, as it's a long story for a beer as it's not something that we like talking about so don't ask something like that is not going to happen again." The captain finished. Not going to happen again? Office feet had two things off his death list. Not a bad day.

Chapter Three

Game of cards?

Ensign Chris and Office Cooper 2nd Lieutenant are in the ships transport heading off into the rest of the ship.

"So how long have you known 1st Lieutenant Dan?" ensign Chris asked. He didn't really care he just wanted to hear the story about the Lords Admiral daughter. He needed to be the first to know this for a number of reasons with the biggest one being to tell the story first to the rest of the crew to get a seat at the card table. Maybe, Ensign Chris was thinking to himself, if I am the one telling the guys about this story, they will let me join the table and play cards like, a hey cool join us, he was thinking to himself. A big smile came across his face just thinking about it, finally they will let me play with them and be accepted by the cool part of the ships crew! He didn't get an answer from Cooper so he asked again.

"Did Office Fett tell you anything about his story with the Lord Admirals daughter?" He asked again needing this information.

"I...I... don't know" Cooper said back. Ensign Chris didn't even hear him he only wanted the gossip. At this point he was in full day dream. Getting a seat at the table was just the start this would mean he could play off ship. Every time the ship docked or was planet side the card crew would jump off find the local game and have the best time of any part of the crew. Chris just wanted that and Cooper was his ticket. He pushed again. "No details at all?" Sounding shocked that he didn't know anything.

"No SIR!" Cooper answered back like the ensign was the higher rank which he clearly was not. This took Chris aback. This Cooper kid was so used to being at the academy even if he did know something, he was not going to say anything. He needed to get Cooper to lighten up. Time to take him the long way round, back off be his friend then rip it out of him!

"Did you see the fighters on the way in?" Now this was a good plan. Academy guys that didn't get into flight school always want to fly. Let see what a space fighter could do.

"No I didn't, SIR!" Cooper barked back.

"You do know you are a higher rank than me? You don't have to call me sir." Chris said with a very confused look. Thinking to himself is this kid stupid or could he just be very nervous being on the Nowhere? God knows what the outside world thinks of this ship. The idea that God did know popped into his head as God often stopped by the ship as one of his best friends was on the crew. This did give him a smile, now just to get Cooper to do the same.

"It's ok" Chris said "I was nervous my first month on this ship. It doesn't run like normal ships" Cooper didn't care or understand because he had never been on a ship before he wanted a bed and to be told his job. At the academy he cleaned things. He was good at that. That was the only job that he could do that didn't get him in trouble.

"Do I get a room?" Office Cooper replied "I mean do I get my own room?" Happy that Cooper finally spoke Chris jump on the words.

"Your very own room all to yourself you can take your pick!" Cooper smiled at this he hated rooming with people they always made him feel stupid. Seeing this smile Chris said "We will get you all set up after a nice look about" Cooper's smile was getting bigger which made Chris think he was getting somewhere.

"On too the docking bay to play with some fighters then!" Chris added. Cooper was now warming up to the idea to play fighter pilot maybe this was going to be his new job?

Back on the bridge 1st Lieutenant Dan Fett was talking with Captain of the Nowhere Captain Cheese.

"Office Fett being new to the Nowhere and my 1st Office second in command of this tub I have some very strict rules for the first 4 weeks." Captain Cheese droned "You will only and I mean only be on the bridge or in your room. Do I make myself clear Fett?"

"Yes Sir! "Fett replied "May I inquire why, Sir." He added.

"Yes officer. This server two purposes. The first and very important reason is your safety. Until you understand how this ship runs, they are the safest places for you. "The Captain was looking deep into Fett's eyes burning the idea that he would die if he didn't follow what he said to the letter. Fett reminded himself he was here to replace his last first Office who died. Could this be the reason? Did the last first Office not follow the rules, is this the reason he died? He was going to follow the rules he needed to get back to Catherine. "The second reason is the longer you don't talk with the crew the more they will respect you. If you become friends with them, they will not listen to you. You only get one shot at building this line of power and it's when you first come into the ship. Following the rules will make your life better on the Nowhere." The captain finished

Fett asked "Where is my room sir?"

"It's not really a room" the captain answered "You have about 6 rooms all together with everything you need" Office Fett liked the sounds of that he could work on trying to get off this ship and back to Catherine without anyone bothering him. Normally a place to sleep and a wash room was all he would get. This might not be that bad. The Captain added.

"If you need anything not in your room ask only myself or Office Spu. Do I make myself clear?"

"Yes Sir" Fett replied. Officers always used that line 'do I make myself clear' it goes over like nails on a chalkboard sending shivers down the backs of Offices who are about to do something stupid or normally just had. It did seem that both officers had come to a level of understanding. The looks on both of their faces made that very clear and, in that pause, Office Spu walked back onto the bridge. Looking right at the captain and spoke.

"All done." "O looks like they are going to the fighter Deck." Spu then looked at Office Fett and said "Cooper and Chris" to clarify who he was talking about. Fett nodded back then asking.

"What level is the fighter squadron at?" Fett needed to start to get an understanding level of what the ship could do in a combat situation after all he was second in command. The Captain and Spu looked at each other like they both had a secret about the fighter squadron. The captain answered.

"Divine squadron is a very capable unit, they normally have three working ships and" at this point Fett jump all over the Captain.

"Only three working ships?" The look on Fett's face was of total shock. Fett looked over at Office Spu who didn't so much as bat an eye over the 9 missing ships or the TWO FULL squadrons also missing.

"I think we need to tell fleet about this right now!" Fett was thinking about the ships class one of its main strengths was the fighter squadrons. No squadrons no strength. This could be a real problem in combat. The Captain said in a very calm voice

"If you need anything you talk to myself or Officer Spu, on this matter about Divine squadron you will have to watch the combat vids to understand" So don't talk to fleet? Fett was starting to think the No-Where had a secret or two he needed to find out. Maybe this could help him get leverage to get off this ship.

"Yes Sir!" Fett answered not caring about the ship not being combat ready just that the leverage behind that was going to help him get off this ship.

Office Spu then looked at the Captain and said "Just get more squadrons jees." Fett could see Office Spu could understand this needed to be done too. Fett might make a friend out of him. The Captain said

"I have sent the vids to your room for you to review, I want you to give me a full report of your findings"

"A report on the combat vids?" Fett asked making sure he understood the task as it didn't sound like a normal report.

"Yes" the Captain answered. "This will serve us both well. As you are new here this will give you an idea of what this ship is about." They both nodded "You will also start to trust me. Show him to his quarters Spu" The Captain finished with a nod to officer Fett. Both Spu and Fett entered the ships transport system and the doors closed.

By this time Cooper and Chris had arrived at the Dock. In Coopers mind he was going to play fighter pilot! He couldn't wait to fly about the Stars this was going to be fun!

"Here we are" Chris said as they both stepped out of the ships transport system to explore the depths of the ships dock. A normal battle cruiser would have up to 3 squadrons of 12 working ships. In addition, each squadron had 2-4 in reserve the mechanics would be working on Thus the space of a dock on a battle cruiser was so big you needed a transport to get around. With that number of ships, you had more than double that in transports to service them. They were lined up all along the wall next to the door of the ships transport system. They had a very smart way of working in which when you took one the system would move the next working transport up the line to the door. This way you knew you always would have a fully working and charged transport to get you about the Dock. No one really came down to the Dock it was an area the fighter pilots had all to themselves. Chris jumped into the first transport yelled at Cooper to jump on and away they went.

"No one really comes down here" Chris started speaking sounding like a tour guide as he was looking around.

"The pilots are not nice to people that are not them"

"Not them?" Cooper said. Confused by the saying. If you are not you, maybe someone put a microchip in your brain to change who you are or maybe a demon got inside you. This train of thinking made no sense even to Cooper who was thinking it. This idea started to scare Cooper he needed to stop thinking about demons now. Thankful Chris answered him which took his mind off demons for the time being.

"I mean not fighter pilots" Chris answered Cooper's question. "The fighter pilots keep themselves away from everyone else, they think they are better that everyone" Chris added.

"Better at what?" Cooper said not understanding the point Chris was trying to make.

"Better at everything, they think and act like they are better at everything than you." Chris now was snaping at Cooper. It was ok Cooper didn't notice which was a good thing because he was really snaping at the pilots. He still just wanted to stick to his plan of getting the info out of Cooper so he would need to keep being nice to him. The number of times the pilots picked on him or put him down made Chris hate them. He hadn't known this until just then, trying to tell Cooper about them. In Coopers brain all he heard was I am going to be a pilot I am going to be better at everything better than everyone else. A big smile came over his face thinking about this. Chris looked over, seeing Cooper smiling made him smile as they raced down the dock. Cooper said

"We didn't land in this dock? I don't think?" Was Cooper talking to himself? Chris's face was a look of total shock. Cooper had said something as he was right even if he was talking to himself.

"Your right!" blurted out Chris. "We have four docks on 2 levels. You came in the jump shuttle only bay." This was the kind of stuff you should be telling someone new to the ship. Helping them to get used to the workings of the No-Where. Well not on this ship. The bigger secrets normally would be covered first for the safety of the new

crew member. The Captain said with the academy scores of Coopers being so low he might not even understand what's going on and Office Fett was not to be trusted. Office Fett was most likely a spy and was left up to the captain to take care of.
"Can you hear that?" Chris asked Cooper.

"Yes" Cooper replied.

"That music is from the fighter pilots" Chris said smiling back at Cooper. Cooper in turn smiled back.

      The transport pulled up to what seemed to be a camping site in a hangar with two guys sitting down around what appeared to look like a space heater. One stood up and spoke loudly.

"Welcome to Alpha squadron!" He had his arms out fully in a cross waiting to give Chris a big hug. The second said in a very calm voice.

"We are not called Alpha squadron that name is so dumb." He didn't look up or move. Chris jumped down from the transport and gave the man with the out stretched arms a big hug. It looked like two old friends meeting again for the first time.

"This is Alpha" Chris said. Looking very happy like he just found his big brother for the first time in years.

"Him sitting down, that's Zig" Chris added. "They are pilots in Divine squadron "

"A, Alpha squadron "Alpha said to Chris with a you must be crazy to think anything else look on his face.

"Alpha stop" Zig said "It's not going to work" Zig spoke very calm and softly but still didn't look up from whatever he was doing. "You can't keep calling it Alpha squadron with the hope we forget we are called Divine squadron and name it after you that's not going to happen."

"This is one of the new guys." Chris said trying to move the conversation away from whatever drama was going on with Alpha and Ziggy. Alpha jumped right in to talk to Cooper who by now had stepped down from the transport and was standing with them.

"Hey new guy, I am Alpha head of Alpha squadron here on the ship."

"So dumb" The soft voice of Zig said shaking his head still looking down at whatever he was doing came from the back.

"Can you fly?" Alpha inquired.

"I'm going to be a pilot!?" Cooper said in a way that no one could understand what he meant. It sounded like Cooper was asking them a question and at the time sounding like a 5-year-old telling you what they wanted to be when they grow up. I'm going to be a pilot!

"So dumb" Zig said softly under his breath. Alpha pushed on.

"Did you fly before?" Alpha inquired again. Maybe this guy is going to join us thinking to himself.

"Yes." Cooper said nodding his head. There was a pause as everyone was waiting for him to tell them what he flew before. Cooper didn't say anything he just smiled looking at them. Alpha pushed on again.

"What did you fly before" Alpha was now wording the question as if he was talking to an idiot not a pilot.

"I flew in the jump shuttle to get here" Cooper said.

"So dumb." again came from Zig who was now laughing to himself under his breath.

"The jump shuttle?" Alpha barked with his voice rising. "everyone has flown a jump ship what fighters have you flown." By now Alpha was starting to lose it. Alpha could and would blow up over anything and the fact he hadn't yet was a surprise. Cooper answered him.

"I didn't fly the jump shuttle I was in it" He babbled still with a smile on his face.

"What!" Alpha yelled "What am I listening to."

"So dumb." was heard again with Zig adding his voice.

"How stupid are you kid?" Alpha had blown. "This is a new level of stupid I didn't know they let people as dumb as you live?" "Hey Jiggb you have to meet this guy!" he yelled out the back to another pilot. Jiggb was out the back in a large hanger room in the dock. A voice came back.

"No, I am busy!"

Alpha carried on "Did you think you were going to be a pilot?" Cooper looked at Chris as it was him who said he could be one. He was going to be the best at everything. Alpha didn't let Cooper answer. "Wow I am going to have to make new ranks of all the stupid people to fit you in."

"I did get the lowest score in the history of the fleet academy" Cooper added like it was an achievement.

"This is so dumb it's starting to hurt" come softly from the back again. Ziggy still didn't look up from what he was doing.

"What!" Alpha screeched "That's a thing. How the hell are you down here with us on this ship?"

"I am showing him around, Captains orders." Chris piped up, to say something like he was defending Cooper. Chris looked over Cooper's way making eye contact to reassure him everything was ok. Hearing the word Captain made Alpha think of rank. The ship didn't respect rank much. It didn't follow the normal military rules they had different rules to follow but this did make him look at Coopers arm setting him off again.

"How the hell are you the same rank as me!?" Alpha voice was now a high pitch scream.

"Has the universe gone retarded? How is a moron like you the same rank as me? I'm done. I'm done" Alpha was saying as he walked in to the big hanger. He stopped looked back at Chris and said "I thought you were an idiot but this guy." Turning to Zig he finished by saying "are we just the only smartest people in the universe? This can't be." He was more talking to himself at this point as he walked into the hangar away from the other 3.

"This is so dumb." Zig said again shaking his head still looking down at whatever he was doing.

"Thanks Alpha." Chris yelled at the hanger door which he had disappeared into. "Later zig." Chris then turned to Cooper putting his hand on Cooper's shoulder saying. "Come on let's go and get some food." walking them back to the transport. Cooper asked Chris. "I am not going to be a pilot?" As they sat down on the transport. Chris's plan had worked perfectly. He was the only one Cooper would trust. As they drove away you could hear a soft voice saying

"So dumb."

Chapter 4
Can I play Cards?

The door opened on 1st Lieutenant Dan Fett's new quarters as he and Office Spu walked in.

"You're going to like it here" Office Spu said walking in just ahead of Office Fett.

"What makes you think that?" Fett asked

"You have 6 rooms all to yourself with everything you could possibly need!" Office Spu said speaking in the same low monotone voice, sounding like he wanted the quarters.

"You have no one close to you to bother you or to take your stuff, simply heaven!" This answer from office Spu seemed completely out of character and he looked like he was about to break into a dance. Spu caught himself whipping his head around fast to see if Office Fett was watching. He was. He made Spu think he wasn't but he was. Office Fett acted like nothing had happened which made Spu have a look of relief on his face. What was Spu hiding? This ship has something wierd going on Fett was sure of it. He didn't care he just wanted to get back to his Catherine. If that meant he had to use Spu or this ship he didn't care he only had one loyalty not to the Fleet, but to the one he loved and he didn't want that secret getting out.

"The hollows of Divine squadron in combat the Captain wanted you to report on are in the computer here." Spu said back in his normal monotone voice as he showed Fett where in the computer to find them. Fett's eyes started to look around the area he now called home. Taking it all in not looking at what Spu was doing. Thinking to himself I know how to use a computer.

"I know how to use a computer." Fett found the words he was thinking coming out of his month again. This has gotten him in trouble before.

"Go on then." Spu replied.

"Computer." Fett opened by using the normal voice command every computer has used for 10,000 years. This time he didn't hear anything? He carried on. "Computer run Divine squadron hollows of the last combat mission." No answer.

"Computer run any hollows of Divine squadron in combat." Still no answer from the computer. Fett looked over at Spu who had his arms folded and a big smile on his face.

"Are you going to listen now?" Spu asked.

"The computer doesn't use voice?" Fett asked with a look of total shock coming over his face.

"Computers don't work with voice." Fett's voice was starting to break. He was looking for some answer from Spu who only said again.

"Are you going to listen now?" Fett didn't and went off again.

"If we don't have voice comms, how do I get food make things I am going to be lost." Now his voice had cracked and his eyes were going back left and right in his head trying to make sense of what was going on.

"Are you going to listen now?" Spu said slower still in the same monotone voice that moment when he let his guard down had gone. Office Fett's eyes looked at Spu's with his mind now broken with the problems this was going to cause him on this ship. How much harder everything was going to be from eating to taking a shower. He was ready to listen.

"Yes, yes I am listening." Fett said looking at the panel on the wall Office Spu was touching.

"This is the hollow panel, here are the files the Captain wants you to do a report on." Office Fett was now listening to every word. Spu continued. "Touch the file you want with your finger and then it brings up a list of controls for that hollow. You can start it with this button stop with this one." Spu looked back at Office Fett to see if he was watching this time. Which he was with his eyes wide open taking everything in. Spu smiled thinking to himself yes bitch listen to me. But didn't say it out loud. "To go back one screen, you hit top left corner. You can do this on all the pads." Spu finished by looking around the quarters arm out pointing at all the panels on the wall.

"Each panel controls an area, over here is food." Spu walked over to the food touch panel to show Office Fett how to use it. Fett was right behind him so as not to miss a thing.

"Evey panel is set up the same way." Spu started to sound more helpful but the monotone voice was still in full effect going on. "The top level gives you options to the next level and so on until you find what you need." "You can always go back a level by hitting the top left conner. The food panel is the easiest to understand. Learn this and everything is easier." Fett looked down at the food panel and could see pictures on the screen of types of food. He could do this it didn't seem that hard. Spu said "Give it ago"

So he did. He hit deserts which gave him a second list full of more pictures. He hit ice cream. Then all of a sudden, a female voice asked. "would you like some ice cream Lieutenant Dan?" Without thinking Office Fett said yes nothing happened. Spu looked at him funny. "Voices can come out but nothing goes in, it's not that hard." Spu mocked him. Fett in frustration hit the back button on the panel.

"I get the basic understanding of it" Fett said to Spu. Fett didn't like to be mocked he had enough of that back on the main worlds with the news about him and Catherine getting everywhere he was mocked all the time. The little things set him off after all the stress the Lord admiral had put him through, he had been pushed to his breaking point.

"I will let you be" Spu start for the door. Fett called over to him.

"How long does it take to learn all of this?" He asked Spu to get an idea of how long he would feel stupid.

"Just learn computer jees!" Spu yelled back on the way out of the door.

Back on the ship transport system Cooper and Chris were making their way to Coopers new quarters. Cooper couldn't wait to have a space of his own. His own room. His very own bed where no one was going to put horrible bugs sand or anything else in it to make his life hell. He had an inner happiness he couldn't remember having before. He never had this feeling previously that he could remember and he was going to hold onto it. Chris also seemed very happy with himself, after all he got the pilots to yell at Cooper, pushing Cooper to only have one friend, him. Office Fett might also be Cooper's friend but Chris didn't care about that, just the story. Which Chris went after.

"How did you like the Dock?" He asked Cooper

"It's very big." Cooper couldn't wait to be a pilot but was worried he would get lost in the dock.

"When do I start flying with all the other pilots?" He asked Chris. Chris couldn't tell him he was not, or every going to be, a pilot that would break Cooper's heart. He answered the only way he could.

"We will have to ask the Captain that's his call" This was the go-to answer for anyone on the ship that didn't want to answer anything, or more to the point totally avoid the question. This was a total avoid the question time. Chris was still trying to get the full story of the admiral's daughter and Office Fett.

"Here we are." Chris said as the transport stopped "Your new home" Cooper looked about and could see a big number on the wall.

"What is that number for?" pointing at the big 55 on the wall.

"This is the number of levels you are on. 5 floors up 5 tracks deep. This is how you find your home." Chris tried to explain the ship numbering system which was very simple and used on every ship since the beginning of time. Taking a look at Coopers face it was clear he didn't have a clue what had just been said. The next thing he said proved it. Very carefully putting his head out of the door. It was like he was scared of something, he said.

"I am scared of heights I can't be up this high!" Now he was holding on to the wall trying not to fall off. Chris closed his eyes and took a deep breath. How was he going to? Wait his guy thinks he can fall from floor to floor. He really is an idiot!

Chris's brain started to work over time. Right, lie, lie about everything he is an idiot and will believe the whole lot. Chris was also thinking that if this kid believes what he is about to say he could get him to do about anything. This could be fun.

"Just think 33 is a magic floor." Chris said to Cooper trying not to laugh. Cooper was still holding onto the wall but was looking at Chris.

"This magic follows around you not the ship. Cooper did they not tell you?" Chris was in full bullshit mode and didn't know where he was going to take this lie, he was doing all he could to stop laughing.

"With this magic you can't fall" Coopers back started to straighten his hands came off hugging the wall. He turned and faced Chris and said only one word.

"Magic" As Cooper said this he looked down at his hands. A big smile came over him. Looks like the falling from level-to-level problem was fixed. Then it hit Chris. With an idiot like Cooper, he would really think he was magic. Chris now needed to fix this problem and not make ten new ones. He got it!

"Didn't anyone tell you this before Cooper?" Chris asked knowing the answer would lead Cooper into his trap.

"No." Cooper answered looking at Chris "no one told me I was magic before, I could tell something was different about me." Cooper went back to smiling at Chris who asked Cooper.

"Why do you think that is?" Chris was going to let Cooper think on this for bit then give him the answer he wanted him to believe.

"Why didn't anyone tell me?" Cooper's answer was of total shock why would people hide this from him? He didn't understand until Chris gave him the answers.

"You see Cooper if you tell anyone you are magic you will lose the power. This means you would fall down all the levels into space." Which couldn't happen however the fact Cooper didn't pull him up on this was amazing. "If someone who doesn't have magic talks to you about it, they can take yours" Sounded like a stupid magic rule but it would stop Cooper talking to anyone about it. Unless they are magic too? Which is never going to happen becomes there is no such thing.

"I understand the rules" Cooper said

"Never a word." Chris couldn't believe what he said. This guy would believe anything! How did he not work out that Chris doesn't have magic and he doesn't fall out into space? Then again why would Cooper think you could fall down the levels of the ship into space in the first place? He was not going to ask this question as it could open a can of worms in Coopers mind, he might never get out of. Time to get him in his room and the information Chris needed out of him.

"This way to your new room Cooper." Chris spoke in a normal voice. Trying to bring everything back to a normal way of thinking and talking.

"I understand the rules" Cooper said again. "and thank you for telling me Chris." Chris smiled it was the first time the little idiot had used his name.

"That's ok Cooper just don't tell anyone." Chris replied.

"I won't, don't worry" Cooper said in almost a sad voice. It seemed he finally had something to talk about that would be interesting, something people would want to hear about, but he couldn't say anything. Sad. Chris tried again to bring everything back to normal by showing Cooper his new room.

"It's the first door on the left." Chris point down the hall.

"Good" Cooper answered "I can't turn right."

The door to Coopers room was about 40 yards away from the opening of the ships transport system. The hallway was big and open like most of the ship. As they moved down the hall noise could be heard from a long way down. Chris could see the noise made Cooper uneasy.

"O that noise is the crew." Chris said before Cooper could make up something in his mind. God knows what he would come up with and the web of lies Chris would need to make up to calm Cooper down. Cooper Smiled at the idea he was part of the crew.

"Are they nice?" Cooper asked. Chris didn't want to take Cooper to meet them just yet as he needed to get the info from him first.

"let's just check out your room first." Chris answered not answering the question at all. Cooper nodded and the walked to the door of his new home. The door automatically opened as all doors do on the ship. When the door opened a message came over the comms. Ensign Chris report to the bridge. Chris and Cooper both looked at each other.

"Don't worry about it." Chris said to Cooper. They both walked into Coopers new room, the automatic lights came on and Cooper could see his room for the first time. All office crew quarters had a main living area with sleeping quarters off to the side. The sleeping quarters had a wash room with shower off the side of that. The kitchen area was at the back with an extra dining area. The standard crew quarters didn't have a kitchen or dining area.

"Look here you have your own kitchen area." Chris pointed out. The kitchen area was only really a food replicator but the added space needed for it made a great sitting area. Chris continued "The ship's crew use the canteen at the end of the hall where you heard the noise coming from." Cooper nodded.

"Ensign Chris report to the bridge immediately!" A voice said over the comm system. Chris and Cooper both looked at each other again.

"Don't worry about it." Chris said. "You know how the foodie works" Chris was praying on this one. Please let the idiot know now to get food.

"Yes" Cooper answered "don't you need to get to the bridge?" He added.

"It's ok it can't be important" nothing is ever that important on this ship but with the Captain calling him twice Chris was thinking to himself, maybe something was going on?

"You never did finish the story about you and Office Fett?" Chris asked Cooper knowing full well he did finish the story he just didn't get the answer he wanted. The comms system kicked back on again.

"Get your fucking ass to the bridge now Chris!!" The Captain yelled over the comms. Cooper and Chris both looked at each other this time Chris was red faced and didn't know what to say.

"I better go" Chris said looking around the room trying not to look embarrassed. He headed for the door as Cooper said.

"Thanks for the help Chris." Chris stopped turned around to salute Cooper who Saluted back both grinning from ear to ear. Chris made for the transport system. Cooper walked out of his quarter's door turned left and headed down to the canteen where the crew was.

Chapter 4 Part 2

The scene on the bridge was not panic, not stress, just 3 people standing around impatiently waiting on the lowest ranked crew member to return to the bridge. On a normal ship the Captain would move on without the ensign but this was not a normal ship and not in normal times with the two new crew mates. The Captain needed to do everything by the book and the book said every one of the bridge crew needed to be present on the reading of new orders from the fleet which meant waiting for Ensign Chris. With the new Office Dan Fett on broad, Captain Cheese could not afford any slip ups. It was the Captains impression that 1st Lieutenant Dan Fett was a spy from the Lord Admiral Miku. Until he could understand the situation completely as to why he sent Feet to the No-Where he was going to do everything by the book. Captain Cheese did not believe he was sent to the No-where over something to do with the Lord Admiral's daughter Catherine, there had to be more to it and until he could tell what was going on he would act as if he was a spy. That's the reason the Captain had put him in a part of the ship no one could be and cut all his access to the ships computer system, dock, flight deck, storage bay and crew. The cancer couldn't infect his crew if he cut it out from the start. This ship had too many secrets to just let anyone run around. The other new crew member Cooper didn't matter. If he could find the flight deck the Captain would be shocked. The Captains biggest problem with Cooper was he didn't want to have to send out search parties around the ship looking for him if he got lost. With that the door from the ships transport side of the bridge opened and Ensign Chris stepped out.

"Ensign Chris" The Captain barked at the top of his voice. "Where have you been! I called you on the comms over an hour ago. Your Ident number didn't go through any doors. You were meant to take Cooper to his quarters and then come back to the bridge where have you been!" This was NOT like the Captain, Chris was thinking to himself. Something was going on like he suspected. Normally Chris would say something funny everyone would laugh and they would move on but something was very off Office Spu didn't even move or look up from the computer screen. Chris just told the truth.

"I took Cooper down to the Flight deck to meet the pilots. I didn't think it would be a problem?" Chris said trying to find out what he did was so wrong? "You don't have Ident numbers in the flight dock?" Office Fett asked the Captain.

"No. it's an old ship." the Captains paranoia was starting to get worse. Was Fett going to keep a log of everything wrong on the ship and report back to the Admiral?

"Makes sense." Fett replied. "is Cooper, ok?"

"Yes, Sir, I left him happy in his quarters Sir" Ensign Chris said. Starting to get the picture of what was going on. The Captain was acting wierd because this office Feet had come on with Cooper. He just needed to play along.

"As you are finally here, I can read the orders from Fleet." The Captain stood tall and proud in front of his Captains Chair with the orders in hand. The Captain's Chair was set at the back of the bridge at the top most point. Both doors to get into the bridge were down steps one to the left and one to the right. The reason for moving the Captain's chair from the middle of the room with the

Captains back to both doors was to stop all the shootings. So many Captains where getting shot in the back from the crew a ship redesign had to be done so the Captain could see them coming. Removing the Captains back from the door was not a bad idea. But you might want to spend more time working out why the crews keep killing the captain instead of hiding him at the back of the bridge. Fleet could have looked into the captain killings that covered a 100-year time period but they found it easier to just move a chair. One thing it did was it made for good grand standing and this was what the captain was doing. He did like the show boating.

"It looks like the Fleet have called us in on a training exercise. They added it would be a good way to test the new crew." This was the very point the captain was thinking about. Feet was a spy. "They also added we haven't done a fleet mission as a ship for some 22 years." This part the captain didn't care about. That sounded normal for this ship. The No-Where didn't really do 'Fleet Stuff' as they put it. That was messy took up way too much time and didn't make any money. Then of course the pay check that fleet sent to everyone every month, as the ship would say that didn't count.

"Training exercise, seems that could be fun" Office Feet said. "After seeing what Divine squadron can do this should be easy!" Office Feet stopped looked at the captain and asked. "You have not done a fleet mission in 22 years?" A look of total shock was on Feet's face. Office Spu and Ensign Chris both looked at each other with a knowing nod and shoulder shrug and a that sounds about right look as everyone knows we don't do fleet stuff. Everyone knows we are not going on this training exercise they are just waiting to see how the captain is going to get them out of it like he always does.

"Office Spu tell the crew." Captain Cheese said with a look at Spu as if to say don't fuck about on the comms like normal. Spu understood.

"We have just been sent orders from the Fleet we are going to meet with the training Fleet for an exercise. Spu out." He added at the end. The captain gave him a disappointed look. Spu looked at the captain with his hand and said "what." As if to say I didn't say anything stupid.

"Contact Fleet and give them an eta based on our current position." Captain Cheese ordered Spu. Office Spu's eyes got very wide. "Shit we are going." Spu thought. The reply to the order would normally be some bullshit answer to fleet to get them out of it. Spu look over at Ensign Chris he too understood what was going on. Ensign Chris jumped into his Chair and started plotting a course to the meeting point.

"9 Days Sir." Chris said looking over to Spu both looking at each other waiting for a joke anything to stop this.

"Let me look at the chart before you send it to Fleet" The Captain ordered.

"You have it now Captain." Chris said right away.

"Ok. I have moved the flight path a little bit to pass this asteroid belt. I think we could use the firing practices before the training. It only adds two days to our trip and puts us under the 15-day travel time. Ensign Chris double check please." The captain said very calmly. Chris looked down at his screen.

"Everything checks out sir!" Chris spoke in a shocked voice. The captain was helping to get the crew ready for the training exercise this was not good.

"Send it Spu." The Captain ordered.

"Done Sir!" Spu said looking over at Chris's station both making eye contact with the eyes doing all the talking. So this is really happening then is what both men were saying to each other. The main reason this was such a big deal is the order of things. The last thing you do as a cadet is join the fleets training exercise. This sets you up ready to join your ship. Ships go through a cycle where after being in dock they are tested. Then deep space tested then the last training exercise before going to the front line. Ships on the way back would go to the dock and the cycle would repeat. This is the normal ship cycle of 90% of ships. You do have ships escorting ships back from the front. Other ship hunting down pirates and normal patrols.   After the No-Where was finished with this exercise, it was to war. This was not going to sit well with the crew and the Captain knew it.

In the canteen the crew were playing cards like normal when the new guy walked in the door. He walked past the door looked in turned back on himself and walked in. From the back of the canteen a loud booming voice came.

"Office on deck!" That was said by Moose, a cyber modified human. Cyber modifications are banned across the universe and very hard to come by. If you could find a Doctor to do the work and with an understanding of the parts the price could buy you your own battle ship. Then you would have to find the parts. Both not an easy task with a price tag so high only the very rich or outlaws could pay.

After hearing the words 'office on deck' the crew around the card table jumped up saluted then all started to laugh and sat back down. Cooper was still looking around to see who the Office was, he realized it was him. The same loud voice came thundering across the room again.

"You must be the new guy?" Moose added a hand signal to his words this time waving Cooper over to the spare chair next to him.

"Yes I am new" Cooper answered. Walking over to the Chair next to Moose.

"Sit, sit down tell us about your stupid ass." Moose said. As Cooper was about to sit down another voice asked.

"Do you play cards?" Cooper looked up to see who asked him this at the same time still trying to sit down. This gave Moose time to kick the chair out from Cooper and make him fall flat on his ass. The whole room erupted into laugher with Cooper laughing to. He didn't see Moose kick the chair out of the way and thought he'd missed the chair because he was looking up. With him laughing at himself Moose did see the fun. The point was to get the Officer mad or upset, if he laughed along with the joke and everyone else it was boring. The laughter calmed down and Cooper pulled the chair to him. Sat down at the card table and asked.

"What you playing?"

"It's a poker game. Have you played before?" It was the same voice that asked him if he played cards. His name tag said. Wait he didn't have a name tag? Cooper answered.

"No, I have never played any card games before. My name is Cooper" He added at the end as he stood up put his hand across the table to shake hands with crew member he was talking to.

"I'm double H." The crew mate said as he shook Cooper's hand. Double H had a very puzzled look on his face. Offices didn't shake hands something was different about this Cooper. The rest of the crew noticed it as well. When a new crew mate especially an Office came on Ship on any Ship, he would pull rank straight away for a number of reasons. Most important reason is this is the way evey Office was trained to act. This was exactly what Office 5'2 did and look what happened to him. The rest of the crew perceived the same thing

Double H did. The normal routine of making the Officers life a living Hell was out the window. Cooper was immediately part of the Crew and the poker crew. Even if he didn't know how to play poker yet.

Moose took it on himself to say who everyone else in the room was.

"Those two clowns over there are Panda and Rush and I'm Moose let me teach you how to play cards. Every time you get a king you give it to me!" Moose had no idea what he just did. He didn't know what an idiot Cooper was. This was going to happen Cooper would hand him the kings. Moose Added.

"Give me your kings and I will give you the cards to win the game!" Laughing as he said it because clearly it was a joke. Cooper laughed along as Double H went over the rules. After the second run through Rush stopped him.

"Just play Cooper. It's the best way to learn."

Everyone didn't want to say Rush was right BUT he was so they started to play. Cooper won the first hand without a clue what he was doing and half the crew letting him win. As he turned his cards over, he said to Moose

"Sorry I didn't have any kings. I didn't think I could win without giving them to you." Everyone Laughed. Cooper was hustling them they couldn't believe it! At that point the Comms channel opened and they could hear Spu say.

"We have just been sent orders from the Fleet we are going to meet with the training fleet for an exercise. Spu out"

Double H laughed. Moose said

"Na this is a wind up, they are not sending us in"

"You heard the man." Rush said.

"I think we should check this out before we all jump to conclusions." Panda said with and added "Just calm down calm down lets find out."

"Ask your friend" Moose jumped in eager to find out if he was going to war again.

"I am not calling him to find out something like this" Panda was almost pissed Moose asked.

"It's more simple than that. GARY!" Panda yelled.

"Good point" Double H said as he laughed rocking back in his chair.

"O Gary!" Panda said again. Cooper asked Moose.

"Who is Gary?"

"Ships lazy ass computer." Moose answered busting into a rage yelling "Wake your lazy ass up Gary!" This confused Cooper Computers didn't sleep? Did they?

"WHATS WITH ALL THE YELL!" The computer was awake yelling back at the people yelling at him.

"Are the ships orders right?" Moose asked.

"What ship orders I don't know anything about ship orders?" The Computer Gary said.

"The orders that just happened! You dumb Fuck." Moose's rage was about to boil over at this point he had given up trying to talk to the computer.

"I DIDN'T GIVE ANY ORDERS THAT'S WHAT I AM SAYING. Fuck." The computer answered back.

"We know you didn't that's not what we are asking." Panda said very Calmly.

"O sorry my bad." The computer replied.

"JUST LISTEN" Moose's rage wasn't over but before he could go full Moose rage Panda put his hand up to stop him.

"The bridge just gave orders did you hear them?" Panda asked.

"No. I was busy doing something." Computer needed to tell everyone the reason why he didn't know something and that it's not his fault.

"Just read the bridge comms back to see what they said" Panda trying to be helpful.

"Good idea, FUCK I can't see the bridge comms" Computer Gary was about to kick off as its what he does best. "Why can't I see the comms from the bridge? Ill BE BACK going to yell at the bridge and find out was going on."

The Comms clicked off then back on with the normal Click.

"WHAT THE FUCK, I AM LOCKED OUT OF THE BRIDGE! THEY DO KNOW I AM GOING TO SUCK THEM OUT AN AIR LOCK. WHAT THE FUCK IS GOING ON!" Computer Gary was not happy about being locked out of anything the ships computer ran the ship, that's the reason it didn't need a crew. Bad accidents happened on the ship if you pissed this Ship's computer off.

"Looks like it's true." Rush said.

"WHATS TRUE!" Computer Gary yelled at everyone "What's going on?"

"We are going to war" Double H said to Gary.

"Do you want to call your friend now panda?" Moose said.

Chapter 5
O Captain my Captain

The bridge was very quiet. The good news was the crew hadn't come to the bridge and killed the captain. This was a strategy common with crews. The idea behind it is that was without a captain they can't do a training exercise. No training exercise no going to war. Fleet would always send a new captain and resend the ship on the training exercise but this would all take time.

Captain Cheese made the smart move of locking the ships computer out of comms on the bridge. With office Fett 'the spy' on the ship it was the last thing he needed. He had kept the office in his own part of the ship for this reason. If Fett talked to the computer, he would report this to fleet and that would be the end of the No-Where. That couldn't happen God would be mad. This could get out of hand and not in the Captains control very fast. Moves needed to be made to keep the crew onside. If the crew wanted it could get out of hand very fast and the captain could lose control of his ship.

"Office Spu" The captain called. "Comm the whole ship. Meeting in 45 mins in the launch Dock."

"Yes Sir!" Spu yelled. Half for the fun of yelling and the rest for still keeping up the act of professionalism.

"Is the crew going to be a problem?" Office Fett asked his captain.

"This crew is never a problem." The captain turned to look at Fett as if to said he was crazy. Of course this was a total lie. Both Ensign Spu and Ensign Chris turned back around to look at the captain with eyes of what the hell this crew is a big problem! You are lucky to still be alive after telling them they are going to war. "I am going to head down now to the dock." The captain said to everyone on the bridge in a strong voice portraying confidence. "Office Fett you have the bridge until I return." The captain walked to the ships transport system and left the bridge. Just after the doors closed Ensign Spu said.

"If he returns" Both he and Ensign Chris stood up and started putting money in a pile.

"What do you mean if he returns?" Office Fett asked with a shaky voice then noticing the ensigns pile of money. "What are you two doing?" Office Fett mind moved from dead captain to pile of money.

"Betting on how many times they are going to shoot the captain." Ensign Chris said in a very calm way. Ensign Spu was looking at Fett surprised that he would even ask them? Of Course, that's what we are betting on. With that look on his face Spu said.

"Feet you better hope the Captain comes back"

Office Feet sat back in the captain's chair with a million thoughts running through his mind is this what happened to the old first office 5'2? Would he be the new captain? How could he get back to his Catherine? Maybe he needed to make friends fast. He needed to join the bet.

"50 on getting shot" Office Feet said.

Both ensign Chris and Spu laughed. Ensign Chris explained the bet.

"It's not if they shoot him, it's about how many times, they shot him." They both laughed again. Spu added

"They are not going to like going to war. Everyone is going to shot the Captain we are really betting on how many times each one does."

"I am out" Officer Feet Said "I don't know the crew to bet on that." He sat back down in the Captains chair with his mind whirling and completely missing the fact Ensign Spu calling him office Feet.

"If the captain doesn't fix this one you are going to get to know the crew real fast." Ensign Chris said.

  In the ships transport system, the captain was coming up with his plan. First, get the crew onboard second, get out of this training exorcise. Both seemed a tall order. The captains first idea was to get to the meeting about 10 minutes early knowing that some of the crew would be there. This would work if he could get some of the crew on his side first. If he couldn't get the first part of the crew understanding he was going to be a dead man. The ship transport system seemed slower than normal which of course it wasn't. It was to do with the dread the captain was feeling talking to the crew. He needed to snap out of it the crew would smell the fear and eat him alive. He came out of his day dream as the doors of the transport system opened to the dock. As he walked past the threshold of the door his face changed from being in a sad mood to totally happy and ready to go. How he just needed to keep the act up in front of the crew. As he walked out, he could see a group of transport carts to get around the dock had been moved. They made a half circle providing a make shift sitting area for the crew. Some of the crew were already here just like the captain had planned. It was Divine squadron and the ships Doctor Harry. Now all the captain needed to do was get them on his side.

"Thanks for coming early guys let me tell you what's really going on." This seemed like a good place to start let them know more is going on than they know.

"We worked that out." Alpha from Divine squadron started in on the captain "Just to let you know we are not going to war!"

"That's my plan too." The captain added trying to stop the talk about war right from the start.

"So what is going on?" Zig asked very calmly and slowly.

"I believe the new Office is a spy from Fleet and this is the reason for the orders. I think Fleet is seeing how we react to the orders then will take steps to remove me as captain." Wow the Captain told himself in his mind. Everything he said was all true and made sense, sometimes I surprise myself was the last thought that came across his mind as he waited to see what the crew's reaction was going to be. It was clear they didn't believe him as they all burst out laughing. All but Harry the Doctor.

"That idiot is not a spy" Alpha said

"Sorry captain I hate to say Alpha is right but Alpha is right." Zig added very calmly and slowly.

"Cooper wanted to be a pilot he is a complete fool Captain. He is not a spy you don't have anything to worry about." Alpha said with total confidence as normal.

"We have a new member of the crew?" Harry asked. "Why didn't I get told I should have his medical records for a start!"

"That's a good point Doc." The captain said not totally understanding why they didn't get sent the moment they landed on the ship. "I will make sure you get them sent over when I get back to the bridge."

"How did you not know we have a new crew mate?" JJB asked the Doc giving him a look of disgust.

"I don't hang around you little people!" Doc Harry said back with his own level of disgust. With the small level of understanding about not going to war everyone seemed ok. Fighting like normal and no one wanting to shoot the Captain. All good signs.

"NOT COOPER!" the captain yelled "Office Dan Fett."

"O" Alpha said looking totally shocked "Not talked to him."

"I didn't know we had a second one." JJB added

"I didn't know we had a first new crew member now two?" Doc Harry added to that.

"I see the problem" Zig said as a noise behind them stopped everything. It was the rest of the crew coming out of the transport system. The first voice was Moose.

"Who's shooting the Captain then?"

With that all hell broke loose. Divine squadron calming down the incoming crew just like the captain planned.

"Shut up and sit down!" The Captain yelled. As everyone made their ways to sit down the normal banter from old friends kicked off. Pushing each other around and mean jokes flew about, everything from losing hair to ex-girlfriends nothing was off the table. The Captain had to jump on everyone again to stop the chatter.

"HEY, SHUT THE HELL UP." The Captain yelled again this time everyone did. "I need to bring you all up to speed with what's going on"

"Good" Panda stepped in "or I call on my friend"

"Do it Panda" Rush egged him on.

"We don't need any of that" The Captain cut them off. "I will tell you what's going on if you all SHUT THE HELL UP." Captain Cheese was starting to lose his cool.

"Ok princess, don't get mad" Moose said bringing the crew chatter to an end.

"The new crew member Office Dan Fett is I believe a spy." He used the Offices full name so the crew didn't think it was Cooper again. "I Believe he was put on this ship to remove me as Captain and you all know what that means for you." The whole crew was very quiet no one looked at each other but only at the captain. "I have the Officer in the first mate's area of the ship only, with no access past the bridge so he can't get into the rest of the ship."

"Are we going to war Captain?" Double H asked. No one could take their eyes off Captain Cheese.

"At this point I don't know. I have made the flight path pass an asteroid belt for a bit of shooting practice. We have 11 days people and it can't be our normal bullshit. Office Fett will see past it."

"Is that the reason Gary is locked out of the bridge?" Moose Asked.

"That's exactly why Gary is locked out of the bridge and why we are meeting here. Gary could 5'2 us all. If Fett worked out, we had the last AI running the ship he would tell Fleet and we would be blamed for the war." The captain finished.

"Then we would all be 5'2ed." Double HH said

"Fett wouldn't think Gary is intelligent? We don't think that and we know him." Alpha piped in.

"That's not what would happen. Gary would start a fight with the Fett at some point over nothing and it would get out." Captain Cheese pointed out.

"What do we say to him then?" Doc Harry asked?

"Yea you know he is going to ask?" Rush pushed Cheese for an answer he didn't want to deal with the bullshit from the computer.

"Just tell him to help me out until we get Fett off the ship. O and point out he can't 5'2 him or we are all in big trouble." Cheese gave them the answer they all needed to have a normal life on the ship. The ships computer, Gary would do this for Cheese no questions asked. If it was not for the Captain Fleet Gary would have been killed long ago. Gary would do anything the Captain asked. Even if it was 5'2ing someone. Thankful the Captain didn't ever ask his crew to do anything like that. Gary would stay in line.

"Is the only problem this Office Dan Fett guy?" Zig said knowing the captain for a long time he would often hold things back from the crew.

"Cheese" Zig said again "it's just this Fett guy, right?"

"Yes" The Captain finally answered.

"Office Feet came on the ship with?" Cooper asked not understanding anything that was going on. "He just wants to get back to his girlfriend. He told me"

"His girlfriend the Lord Admiral's daughter this makes total sense now." With his eye brows up Alpha had put the same dots together the captain did and came up with the same answer.

"Miku hates you." JJB said looking around at the rest of the crew now fully understanding what the Captain was thinking.

"He would love this ship back" Panda to was deep into the understanding of how this was going to end.

"Let just kill him then." Double HH said not understanding why he couldn't just do that.

"We can't" Moose answered before the captain could. "There would be an investigation and they would take the ship."

"They didn't all the other times?" Double HH didn't get it yet.

"All the other times the people were not the Admirals daughter's boyfriend." Zig pointed out

"So?" Double HH's line of thinking was different. "I bet Miku wants this Dan dead anyway. He wouldn't look into why. We are doing him a favor." Double HH finished his point standing up pointing his arms shrugging his shoulders. Was he wrong?

"What would his daughter do?" Zig asked Double HH seeing if he could put the dots together himself. Looking at him hard as if the harder he looked the more help he was giving him.

"Cry?" He answered back not seeing what he meant. Zig helped him out.

"She will make her Daddy investigate the death of her love. He gets a dead guy he doesn't like and the ship." Zig looked at him to see if it had sunk in yet.

"O, he's getting everything he wants no matter what we do" It hit Double HH and he looked at the Captain who was waiting for the crew to catch up. Cheese worked this all out in about a sec and a half after the training orders came in. He was happy the crew worked it all out by themselves. That way it seemed like he hadn't pushed the idea on to them himself.

"I will find a way but for now we follow orders" Cheese had finished the first part of the plan. Somehow, he needed to pull the second part together. "If anyone has ideas how to get out of this training exercise, they need to let me know now. When I go back to the bridge, we can't talk of this face to face again. The rest of the bridge crew doesn't know what I have told you and we need to keep it that way." The captain looked around the very smart and resourceful crew with the hope that the mind power of the group could come up with something.

"We COULDDD call Panda's friend?" Alpha asked looking over at Panda. Everyone looked at Panda for an answer.

"Panda do you think he would? No ship no you." The captain said. Never asking him for help before the crew knew this means this is real and the captain really is stuck. That's how bad it was a sinking feeling could be felt as Panda didn't answer. He had his eyes closed like he was concentrating on something. Talking with someone. He was clearly thinking. The dark silence that fell over the crew was broken as Panda spoke.

"He's not going to help us he can't." The crew sunk just a little deeper. "It's the rules stopping him not him not wanting to help and anyway he is not talking to me at the moment so it's not a good time to ask for anything."

"No Panda help, shit we are fucked then." Moose said without his normal happy laugh at the end of speaking.

"You know we can't bluff our way out of the training it's too easy. They made it to find crews like us. If we are going to go to war nothing hits us. When we get to the asteroid field, I want full game face lots of fire power lots of hitting big rocks. Then the smaller ones. Then the even smaller ones. Until nothing is left. I want this to be the first scar we put on the maps of the universe. This is where the Crew of the No-Where will be remembered. We will blow up everything so they will have to rewrite the star chats we pass through." The captain didn't really believe that but needed something to get his crew going and there is nothing better than blowing things up with this lot. The crew slowly stood up looked around each other nodding heads and hitting each other on the shoulder knowing it's going to get messy from here.

"We got you Captain." Came from Zig

"Yea you always got our back we got yours." Alpha said pulling the whole group together.

"**DISSMISSED**" The Captain said as he stood strong turned around walk back to the transport system back to the bridge.

Chapter 6

Worrying Times

Everything was very quiet waiting for the captain to come back, or his body brought to the bridge. After the captain had left to talk with the crew about the coming war, the two Ensigns had time to think. This left them in a place where the only outcome would be the end of the ship if they lost the captain. The two Ensigns text comm each other trying to work out what happens if the captain dies. The outcomes worked out to be Feet running the ship then war, or Feet running the ship with death or just death. At no point with the captain gone did the outcome look favorable for them and the rest of the crew. In the back of the minds of both Ensigns was all the times the captain tried to move them up the ranks. If only they listened one of them would be first Office and this Feet problem wouldn't be here. The lazy happy do-nothing life style of the whole crew had come back to bite them and this was a shock. They never had to pay for anything they didn't do before. Not being responsible for anything was one of the best parts about being on the ship. When something got to a level someone needed to fix everything the Captain always did it. He had a way of always being in the right place at the right time to pull the crew through. The times he didn't it was like an act of God saved them. This time they could have fixed the problem by stepping up to the job when the captain asked them, not running off to get drunk on the next pleasure planet as the ship docked for 'repairs. They had both let themselves, the crew, and the captain down. They needed to stop worrying about the past as it was all wasted energy they couldn't get back. Ensign Spu told Ensign Chris this in Text.

'Don't look at the past, put your energy into the future we know we both fucked up'

'You are right Spu' Chris text back. The reason for talking on text was so Office Feet couldn't understand what was being said. They both didn't trust him; they didn't have a good reason not to. It was just the normal way everyone on the ship acted. The ship secrets were closely guarded from one crew to the next. Only the trusted people stayed on the Ship. The rest were got rid of like the rest of the trash in space. With no warning the door from the transport system opened and the captain walk back onto the bridge.

"Captain on deck!" Office Feet called. Both Ensigns turned to salute Cheese with big grins on their faces.

"What are you two idiots looking so happy about?" Cheese Asked.

"No one shot you SIR." Chris answered.

"No one is going to shot me on this ship Chris. Did you worry about me?" Cheese asked in a voice making fun of Chris for caring about his wellbeing.

"He didn't care about you he just lost a bet." Office Feet said to the captain. Cheese couldn't tell by the tone of Feet's voice if he was being funny or trying to score points telling on the Ensigns. Cheese walked over to the Ensign picked up the pile of money and spoke.

"I know. I bet I would be just fine. I know my crew." Cheese smiled, Feet did to.

"I am happy you do, the last thing I want is to be Captain of this Boat." Feet said with a smile on his face which was quickly wiped off because all three-crew shut him down very fast.

"DON'T EVER TALK BAD ABOUT THE SHIP"
Spu was the first to yell at him

"Say what you want about us never again say anything bad about the ship!" Chris added

"This ship is your life you will do well to remember that." The captain was the last to put him back line.

"I didn't mean anything by it!" Feet was just as fast to defended himself. "Let me level with you I just want off this ship to get back to my Catherine." This seemed to come out of left field and the captain would use it to see what he could find out.

"Is this your whole plan?" Cheese Laughed at him knowing he is a spy.

"I had to choose, jail or here. I think the Admirals plan was to put me some place Catherine couldn't find me. I miss her. You will tell me if she sends me a message?" Feet said sounding like a broken-hearted school kid.

"You going to be OK Feet?" Cheese asked at the same time having respect for the acting skills Feet was showing.

"It's Fett Sir" Fett correcting the Captain and feeling sorry for himself.

"Of course, it is. Sorry Fett." Cheese was not going to get it wrong again he told himself. "I need you ready to fight Fett, is this going to be a problem?" Captain Cheese didn't need the Spy to help the ship fight. This crew was a well-oiled machine when it came to fighting, the main problem was getting them to do it. It's not that the crew was lazy it's just they didn't see the point because they know they were going to win the fight anyway so why move from the warm bunk or fun card game.

"I am Sir, I am good anywhere you put me I can also pilot a fighter. Nothing like the fighter pilots you have. I looked at the vids of them in combat I have never seen anything like it, Sir." Fett told the captain.

"They are one of many little secrets we have on this ship." Captain Cheese had been on the ship so long he had forgot half of them.

"How do they disappear in full flight and at full speed?" Fett hadn't seen or heard of tec like this from either side in the war. "Did it come from the other side?" Maybe Fett hadn't heard about it.

"No, no its very old tec from the Vancars." Cheese couldn't see the harm in telling him a couple of the Secrets that go on aboard the ship. A simple vid of any battle would show what they have anyway. If he could understand it.

"I have never heard of the Vancars? Who are they?" Fett asked not knowing if this was real.

"They are a very old race around at the start of the universe, they stop by from time to time to help us out, if you are around long enough." The captain was looking at Fett saying the last part. Seeing if Fett was shaken in anyway. He wasn't he didn't even seem to notice what the captain said.

"That doesn't answer anything it just brings up more questions. How did you interface their tec with ours? What does the Tec really do? I can see they disappear and move but how?" Fett's mind was running away with ideas he didn't have any answers to. The captain needed to fill everything in for him.

"Sit down Fett I will tell you what I know about the Blink Tec as we call it." The Captain sat in the Captain's chair at the end of the bridge and turned it to the 1st offices chair waiting for Fett to sit down. He did and didn't sit down at the same turning to the captain.

"I am all ears" Fett said. Cheese spoke.

"I will tell you what I can and no more." Fett was sharp and picked up on the word play the Captain was using.

"Tell me what you can? Not what you know?" Fett asked.

"Yes." Cheese said looking a Fett not giving in to being called out.

"What I can tell you is the Vancar gave the Blink Tec to us as payment for something the ship did for them. We put the Blink on the fighters. The integration of everything was done by Arthune and a friend of the ship." The Captain didn't build on any of the points he made.

"Ok can you tell me what it does?" Fett Asked the Captain.

"As far as the rules go it changes what it does." Fett cut the Captain off.

"That can't be right rules don't change about what technology does?" The face of Captain Changed.

"O, I forget Vancar Technology 101 at the Fleet academy told you all the rules, about a race you just found out about and somehow know what it does. Are you finished?" Cheese did think Fett was a bit of a know it all but never about new tec he had just found out about.

"Sorry Sir I was just thinking out loud." Fett did in fact look sorry. The Captain Carried on.

"As I was saying the rules Change but it always has a cool down timer after its used. The cool down timer is the main thing we have seen change. It was 14-16 seconds now about 20-24 Seconds we don't know if its because we have used it more or that's just the way it is so we go with it." Office Fett didn't know what to think he just asked what came to mind.

"Where do they go in the time they blink? Do they freeze in time let the space move then unfreeze?" Fett asked trying to sound smart but also having no idea what was going on.

"No idea, your guess is as good as any." The Captain looked like he was telling the truth Fett turned and said a of the cuff remark.

"GOD knows then?"

"NO, NO he doesn't." Spu answered.

The Captains face didn't change or give anything away just yelled at Spu to mind his business.

"Keep you mind on your work not on the Offices talking behind you ensign." The captain said not taking his eyes off Fett to see if he picked up on the God comment. He didn't.

"How far do they move forward in space?" Fett wanted to know everything he could about this tec not because it was alien in origin but because if he had a thing, tec was it. He needed to meet this Arthune.

"They blink forward a set distance they know where they are going to come out." Well as far as the captain knew.

"How do they know the distance and what happens if they hit something? Fett wanted to try this out for himself at some point.

"The just know the distance it's a skill level thing its why Divine squadron is the best I have ever seen." Cheese hadn't seen anyone come close to what the guys could do. They can easily deal with 20-1 odds, and the ship hasn't been in a bigger fight yet. Who knows what they really can do?

"If we are going to war, they might be the best asset we have. I take it you have a plan SO we don't go." Fett asked the captain.

"I don't have a plan" Cheese answered. Even if he did, he would not be telling Fett anyway.

"But that means." Fett said

"Yes, war." Cheese butt in

"No, no it means I won't get back." Fett shouted he just had a one-track mind. To get off the ship back to Catherine. The captain was starting to see that. "You must have some idea how to get us out of this training and slow everything down again?" Fett was almost pleading with the captain. It was very sad.

"The only thing I can think of is some hull damage but nothing can hurt this ship. With the added upgrades we would have to have 15 full battle ships hitting us and Fleet would know that it would be a set up to get out of going to war."

"It's sad that we know the next jump gate is a training battle field then the one after it the front line." Fett was thinking out loud of the fate before them."

"Yep, or they hunt you and your ship down like pirates." Cheese joined in feeling sorry for himself.

"Spu" The Captain yelled. "Tell the crew we will be at the asteroid field in 16 hours. Tell them to get some rest and be fully ready for full combat training then. You better add they need to be sober and that's everyone. With that the Captain started to walk off the bridge. He turned back to say.

"Wake me in 14 hours the bridge is yours until then Fett."

Chapter 7

The Spy is Found

Captain Cheese woke to the whole ship being on red alert. The room lights were flashing red with buzzers going off. He wanted a wake-up call but this was a little over the line. A normal Captain on a normal ship would immediately comm to the bridge to find out what the hell was going on. This ship wasn't any of those things so Cheese checked the time. It was the exact time he asked to be woken up so everything was ok. The noise might be a bit loud and seeing was ok with the red flashes so he got in the shower seeing how long it would take for it to stop.

    In the shower it was somewhat tranquil with the lights flashing and the extra loud beep of the emergency buzzer as it echoed around. It was all cancelled out by the warm flowing water. It was like being in a little safe area as the world around is going mad. Maybe I should hurry up and find out what is going on? Cheese had the thought pop in his mind and then he let it go just as fast.

"They can deal with it." He said out loud to himself as he got out of the shower. After drying himself and getting dressed. He sat down for a coffee a good 20 minutes after he woke up thinking to himself 'they should have turned it off by now'. Captain Cheese was going to wait finish his coffee then head to the bridge but when sitting down having the time to think about it maybe he should find out what was going on. So with coffee in hand, he walked over to the transport system and headed to the bridge. The door of the transport system opened to the bridge and over the buzzing and alert noise Cheese could hear the laughter of Ensign Chris and Ensign Spu. As he walked fully on to the bridge, he could see Office Fett sitting in the captain's chair hitting buttons.

"Good morning, all" Captain Cheese said to the crew with a big smile on his face. He couldn't wait to hear this one. He didn't want to ask them what was going on, that would seem needy.

"Captain!" Chris said as he stood up and saluted him.

"Morning Captain." Came from Spu but it was more laughter than words. The captain turned to

Fett who still pushing buttons he hadn't looked up at any point. This is going to be where the problem is then the captain told himself.

"Morning Office Feet" The captain used the nickname Feet hated to shock him out of whatever trance he was in. It didn't work. Feet just carried on trying to do whatever he was doing. Cheese turned back to the two Ensigns.

"Care to explain?" Cheese asked them both as he took a sip of his still hot coffee. The red lights and the buzzing were starting to get on the nerves of the captain who all in all was a patient man. The rest of the crew must be going mad!

"He made a bet he could find Comms button to turn it off Sir." Chris always following orders said to the captain. Cheese guessed as much that something stupid was going on. For office Feet not to look up this had to be a big bet.

"How much money did you take from him?" Cheese asked both ensigns still sipping his coffee.

"We own him." Ensign Chris said looking at Ensign Spu with a big smile.

"HOW MUCH." The captain asked again about the bet. It was normal on this ship to bet. Gambling was banned by Fleet on ships because it could get out of hand. If a lower rank won a bet with a higher rank, it could make problems for that lower ranked person. Just to name one way it could go wrong. Deep in space, crew would kill over bad bets and cheating. Fleet stopped all of the problems with simply banning all gambling. If Feet was gambling with the crew that meant he had broken Fleet rules. This was something Cheese liked.

"We own him captain." Spu finally answered. "This bet is for a total of 5 years of all money he makes" Spu had a big smile on his face as he and Chris looked at each other.

"And what was this bet for?" Cheese asked

"That he couldn't find the off button on the captain's chair." Chris started to giggle again.

"Any idea why the rest of the crew is not going insane with the noise for the last 30 mins?" The captain said as he finished the last of his coffee.

"That's the first thing I stopped Sir, its only on the bridge." Spu said trying to act smart.

"Not in my room" Cheese's face showed he was not amused. This was going to come back on Spu.

"A. I am sorry Cheese, but you did want a wake-up call." Spu was doing Spu things trying to blame everyone else but himself.

"Captain if it's been going off in your room for the last half hour why didn't you contact the bridge?" Chris had a very good point. The captain didn't have a good answer or really want to have to answer Chris so he walked over to his chair removed the panel on the right arm put in the secret captain's code and turned off the horrible noise.

"BETS OFF BETS OFF" Feet started yelling as soon as the noise stopped.

"You lost we own you for 5 years Feet" Spu said

"Yep" Chris piped in for back up. The captain was just standing there. Not sure what to make of the situation. This uptight Office of the Fleet was acting like one of his crew. Maybe it's just because he has not seen the Captain was on the bridge yet. So it's time he did. Cheese spoke

"You lost." he had a smile on his face half laughing like he would normally do with the rest of the crew.

"I didn't, you stopped it before I had a chance!" Feet was talking to the captain like the other members of the crew did almost yelling at him. The normal crew didn't do rank within the ship crew. It was more a family that did everything not to follow Fleet orders and do what they wanted to. What had gone on in the past couple of hours when he was resting?

"Not my problem not my bet." The captain didn't bother to look at Feet. "Now what's going on."

"We are at the asteroid field Sir." Spu said straight into work mode. "Divine squadron have been out blasting crap for about 30 clicks or so."

"Good, good. Anything else to report?" Cheese walked over and threw his empty coffee cup down the trash. Feet was still standing with mouth open waiting to say something about the bet he just lost.

"I don't think so Sir." Spu answered. "Nothing coming in from the guys below deck. I think they will be ready to mount deck guys as soon as you give the word."

"Great work guys." Cheese said as he walked back to his chair to sit down. At that moment Feet could no longer hold back.

"Are we not going to talk about the bet being void?"

"It's not void." Spu said. Then the captain calmly turned around and spoke.

"The way I see it you bet you could find a switch to turn off the emergency alert. You didn't. You lost the bet they own you. Did I miss anything?"

"NO" Chris said as fast as he could.

"That's right we own him." Spu added

"That's not fair! "Feet cried

"It's not about being fair its about winning." Cheese pointed out.

"But." Feet didn't have anything to say. He didn't know what to say. They owned him. What was he going to do?

"What did we learn?" Cheese was talking to Feet like you would a small child. Cheese waited for Feet to answer him. "What did we learn?" He said again.

"Don't bet." Feet answered thinking that's what the captain wanted to hear.

"No, don't lose when you make stupid bets." Cheese was looking right at Feet. Right into his eyes. Deep into his soul. Making a point. Feet didn't know what to say but he wanted to. He didn't have an answer. He didn't know what to do. Then a message hit the bridge.

"We have a P1 comms link for the captain level 7." Spu told Cheese. This gave Feet the perfect chance to turn and run to his room like a spoiled child. With the stamp of his foot, he was gone.

"Level 7?" Cheese said out loud. "I didn't know we had a level 7 did you guys?" Looking around at the rest of the crew. Both shook their heads.

"It can only be opened in your quarters Sir. I just looked it up." Chris was always looking things up. Mainly because he forgot everything.

"Thanks, I will head to my quarters right now, then."

It wasn't long before Captain Cheese was back in his quarters. He had no idea what could be this important. He had a level of excitement it was hard to explain. On the one hand it was like unwrapping presents on Christmas morning, that you can't wait to see but on the other hand it felt like getting into trouble and waiting to be told off. He opened the door and went straight to the comms panel. The incoming message was flashing away waiting to be picked up. Click. Cheese answered it.

"This is a Level 7 message for Captain Cheese of the S.S. No-Where. Scanning for other personal in the room" Cheese didn't even know you could initialize a scan from a message. He looked around the room watching as a wave went around checking everything. The computers voice came back.

"Scan complete. Message ready to relay." The next voice that came on was Lord Admiral Miku himself.

"Captain Cheese this message and mission is something never to be talked about and no history is to be recorded of it or your actions. In the replicator you will see two items. The first is to be put into Office Fett's fighter. The second item is a code to call special weapon systems control. This must be done when Fett is flying 20 clicks or more away from the ship, for the safety or your ship. Fail to perform this task will remove you and your crew from Fleet and have you all labeled as pirates to be hunted down. Picking up both items off the replicator is the sign you have accepted this mission. No other contact is to be made and you must stay with all current orders. End of message" Captain Cheese walked over to the replicator looked at both items and picked them up. The item he was going to put into Fett's ship was a little box.

It had nothing special looking about it or any marks on it no "on" button nothing. It was just a little black box. He could tell that was the item he was to put in the ship because the other one was just a card with a code on it. Well a number and a code. It said send this code number TH427 to number 867-0223 special weapons. He put them in his pocket and headed back to the bridge.

"Well, I guess this is now happening." Cheese said out loud as he headed back to the bridge.

Back on the bridge Spu and Chris waited for the return of the captain. Both couldn't wait to find out what the level 7 message was about. The captain didn't hide anything from the crew he was not going to this time. Was he? As he entered, they both jumped on him Spu was the first.

"What's the deal captain did they pull training and send us on a secret mission?" It was now clear they both just wanted to know if the order to go to the training exercise was being changed.

"Yea are we going on a secret mission?" Ensign Chris sounded excited about where, new orders he had made up in his head.

"We do not have new orders we are to go to the training mission as planned." The captain did take a minute and think about whether or not he should tell the crew. Talking out options with the crew was always something he did to find the right answer. They never gave it to him but just talking out loud helped him work out his problems. This time it felt off to talk with them. This was clear Admiral Miku wanted to assassinate Fett and if that was true, he was not a spy. If he wanted Fett dead why not do that on the way to the No-Where? Why bring Cheese into this at all? This opened up more and more questions about what the real goings on were. Cheese was being played as a pawn in some chess game, he didn't even know was being played. His next move needed to be smart. Telling the crew was not a smart move. If he wanted the game blown up, he would just tell the crew but not now.

After hearing the orders of going to training hadn't changed Spu and Chris lost all interest in what was going on with the new orders. The captain needed to stay on point about what he was doing to get ready for that. If you changed or acted differently the crew would spot that and maybe pull this new secret mission out of him and he didn't know what that could mean in the long term. So stay on point he did.

"What's Divine squadron looking like out there?" The captain asked trying to get back to something that was normal training to keep his mind off the new information he received.

"Not sure what they are doing Sir." Chris answered. Chris not knowing was normal, but he would ask or find the answer just saying he didn't know was something he did not to sound stupid to the captain. People would look down on him call him stupid so he worked out if he didn't know he would find out.

"Not sure? What does it look like?" Cheese asked as he walked to sit down in the captain's chair.

"It looks like they are trying to blow up every asteroid in an area." Chris said back to the captain with his hands up in the air giving him his best guess.

"Why don't you just ask them?" The second the words came out of the captain's month he knew how stupid it sounded. This was confirmed by the way both Spu and Chris turned to look back at the captain with a you know why look on both their faces. Divine squadron was not the easiest lot to get along with. Having to answer questions about what they were doing wouldn't go down well. They might even start shooting at the ship. It had happened before. It was best that only the captain talked to them.

"Open comms Spu. I will ask them myself" Cheese said.

"Channel open, Sir" Spu answered

"Divine squadron care to explain what the hell you are doing?" Cheese said in a joking tone. Zig answered.

"JJB said he was a better pilot that me so" Zig was cut off by JJB.

"Na Na Na that's not what I said. I said I could shoot more asteroids that you." Then zig cut JJB off

"That's saying you are a better pilot that me."

"NO, it's not zig it's saying I am a better shot!" JJB was staying hard on his point. "that's why I said I am a better shot and not a better pilot."

"Being a better shot is all about the skill to be in the right place to shoot. If you are not in that place to make that shot its not about the shot but the skill of the pilot. So, you are saying you are a better pilot than me." Zig said in his very normal calm manner

"Its not" JJB went back at him again. "I Don't need to be in the right place to shot because I am a better shot that you."

"Stop Stop" Alpha jumped in over both of them.

"The captain asked what you are doing not why you are doing it. Right captain?"

"That is what I was looking for." Cheese didn't know he had walked right into the age-old fight of who is the best pilot which all fighter squadrons had.

"As there is no clear way to work it out." Spu jumped in on comms

"Yes, there are even I know that. Just 1v1 with soft weapons? Whats the problem?" Spu seemed shocked that this was not the first thing they tried to do.

"We are not doing that. That's stupid." Answered JJB knowing Zig was the better 1v1 pilot.

"That not the point we are making and I have done more 1v1 practices than JJB so it's not a true test." Zig said pointing out a fact everyone else already knew.

"Can I get back to what I was saying?" Alpha seemed pissed it was always him getting cut off. "I came up with the idea that we pick an area in the asteroid field the same size and clear everyone."

"You didn't come up with the idea Arthune" Zig corrected Alpha.

"My idea" Alpha was still going with it hoping no one would notice. "My idea was to shoot them down to nothing. That way it's the speed of flying shooting all kinds of different skills being used. Good test Huh?"

"Not now the captain stopped us to talk."

"I didn't stop" Zig answered JJB

"That's not fair!" JJB shouted

"I didn't think you would stop shooting" Zig answered half laughing at JJB knowing now he would clearly win. "Why would you stop shooting?"

"The test is rigged, I am done." JJB went to his default of its not my fault you cheated.

"Stop being a baby we can start again." Zig was more that happy to restart and beat JJB fair and square.

"Wait," Cheese said "I have an idea. How good do you think the 3 of you really are?"

"We are the best that's why we are called Alpha squadron." Alpha answered.

"We are not Alpha squadron." Zig was very firm with his words. "We can kick you out of DIVINE squadron and you can start your own with your own ship." Taking the fully modified ship off someone and putting them in a normal ship was not just a cruel thing to do it would be a death sentence. Not having all the extra ways to get away from people, the extra fire power, would make death an easier thing to come across. After the brief silence zig asked.

"What do you have in mind captain?"

"We could do the same idea clearing the asteroids but this time you V us. What do you think?" Cheese answered.

"You mean the No-Where V Divine Squadron? I Guess we could do that." Zig answered in an interested tone.

"That's not fair they have more guns than us!" JJB whined about something again no one listened.

"Are we going to put a bet on it?" Zig asked the captain.

"No not after today the ensign's here own the new office Feet so no betting for a while." Cheese gave both ensign's a death stare. They didn't care no one was going to take the smiles of their faces.

"Office Feet? I thought his name was Fett" Alpha added.

"It is we get it wrong from time to time here." Cheese told Alpha.

"Get it wrong, more like take the piss" JJB said under his beath so no one on the comms could hear. He felt like people did that to him. They didn't but it didn't stop him from feeling that way sometimes.

"Let me get the crew ready and you guys work out which area we are going to take." The captain hoped this could be fun, now it was going to be.

"Cheese" Zig said over the comms "Do you want to run a scan of the asteroid field some of the asteroids we blow up really blow up. I don't know what metals or rocks they are made out of do you want to check in case we blow ourselves up?"

"No." Cheese answered "The check will take longer than the time it will take to blow them all up. We will run a ship scan for a safety check"

"We are always running a ship scan?" Chris told the captain in a very sarcastic voice. "I am sure you should know this being the Captain, but we are always running a ship scan?" Chris and Spu laughed they didn't get to take shots at the captain very often, so they loved it when they could.

"Wait…. So are we going to blow up?" JJB asked with no idea what they were talking about he spent the time when the captain and zig were talking picking the music he was going to play as he blasted stuff.

"We are not going to blow up Jig" Zig said to JJB using one of his many nick names.

"Keep the channel open Spu we might as well tell everyone on the ship at the same time." The captain said.

"Yes sir" Spu answered. "Ready when you are Sir."

"Ok listen up everyone this is your captain speaking" Cheese bellowed out. Chris turned to Spu and said in a funny tone moving his head as he spoke.

"Oh he sounds very captain like today. Doesn't he." They both laughed. The captain carried on.

"We have arrived in the asteroid belt for some shooting training before we get to the main exercise." Every body knew the fleets training wasn't training so the captain needed to do as much as he could beforehand. The fleets idea of training was sitting about and working out who they would be sending where on the front line. The captain spoke again.

"Divine squadron have come up with a little game to make it more fun. We are both taking areas of the asteroid field and it's going to be a race between the No-Where and Divine squad to see who can clear the area the faster. This is everything in that area every big, little and tiny speck of rock. All asteroids need to be destroyed. I want ships that come though this area of space looking at the charts and saying they are wrong because there is no asteroid field left." The captain finished his speech to a lot of chatter on the comms. The best that could be made out was everyone seemed ready to go. With everyone talking at the same time it was hard to make out. Having all the channels open wasn't a good idea.

"One last thing." The captain forgot to tell them all. "We can't use Gary, maned guns only. "After that Cheese called loudly "Battle stations!" Hitting the red alert button. It didn't go off so he hit it again, and again. "Why is this not working?" Cheese asked his two ensigns.

"You turned it off on the bridge with the over ride Sir." Spu pointed out.

"That's right. Its on in the rest of the ship, right?" The captain asked.

"Yes, just not here and your quarters, Sir." Chris replied to the captain.

"That works, back on main comms Spu." The captain ordered.

"I never turned them off?" Spu said questioning back. "If you want that you need to say that. Jess captain." Spu was now looking at the captain with his face screwed up questioning if he was ok. Cheese carried on like nothing had happened. He was not going to acknowledge his mistake. If he didn't acknowledge it, it didn't happen.

 "We are going to have a countdown to the start of the firing after we have received the areas of attack." Cheese looked over to Spu for him to answer. He contacted Ziggy who was ready to send over the areas out lined. Spu in turn sent them out ship wide.

"All done Cheese. Weee are ready to blast." Spu was back in normal crew mode. Cheese let it slide just giving Spu a look.

"Comms still linked." Cheese knew they were he was just checking before the final count down. Spu didn't Answer ensign Chris did.

"Someone is firing Sir!" Cheese's mind flicked on. Who would be cheating?

"Jig stop shooting!" The captain yelled over the comms. He got a response.

"What? I was just checking if my guns are working?" With that a cry of

"Jigs cheating." Came across the ship's comms.

"A, Captain the ship is shooting at jig," Chris reported. At the same time he got a ping on the scanner that was always scanning. He didn't think anything of it with the fire power going off in the back ground.

"You fools can't hit me!" Jig said back as all comms channels were still linked.

"Everyone stop shooting!" Cheese ordered. He had hoped this would go off as a simple training exercise then he remembered his crew. Nothing was simple nothing was going to be easy and everyone would fight him on everything. All of the time. O how he loved his crew.

"I haven't told you to fire yet! And you can't shoot at each other! I shouldn't have to make this a rule but NO SHOOTING each other's ships!" Cheese was in a rant when a voice came back.

"He said ships we can shoot each other" It was clearly Moose pushing the captain mainly because it was funny.

"NO YOU CAN'T SHOOT EACH OTHER. That shouldn't be something I need to say. EVER! Everyone answer me yes Sir!"

"Yes sir." Came back on comms very softly. Cheese was not going to let the weak response stand so he pushed back for a better response.

"I didn't hear you!" He yelled back taking control of his crew. He didn't like to lay the law down but he would if he had to. A louder answer came back.

"YES SIR."

"Good now let's get started. On my count down let's get started. 3…...2……1……. blast away!"

The comms went quiet with everyone on point doing the task set to them.

"Spu cut comms and update me on anything that is going on I need to know." The captain sat back in his chair thinking to himself it can't be that hard just to run a simple exercise? This crew could do anything and have in the past they seem only to fall short on the simplest of tasks.

Chapter 8

Pirates!!

After 2 hours of blasting asteroid after asteroid nothing of note had happened. The race to shoot everything the eye could see was a slow one. Blasting big to small, small to gone was slow. However, this did give the captain time to think over the message he got from fleet. Cutting out the fleet talk this was nothing more than an assassination of Feet. This couldn't just be over the admiral's daughter they would have killed Feet back at home world before he got here. Cheese came up with over 100 ways to do it and make it look like an accident and he didn't have the resources the Lord admiral had. Something else was going on clearly. With a little more time Cheese's big brain would work it out. After all it was something about sending them to war that too would kill Feet. Was it about Fleet taking out the No-Where? Before Cheese could move that idea around in his head for a couple of minutes Ensign Chris popped out with something useless to say.

"Sir,"

"Yes Ensign."

"I think I have spotted something funny going on." This was going to be a first for Chris if he had so the captain didn't pay it much mind but he asked anyway it was the captains thing to do.

"Who is cheating?" Cheese asked. That seemed like the most likely answer to anything that was going on.

"No sir no one is cheating, the scan keeps going off." Cheese was a bit shocked that no one was cheating after a couple of hours. He was sure someone was they just hadn't found them yet.

"The scan that's always run?" The captain asked trying to sound smart. Both ensigns knew the captain didn't know they ran that scan or what it scanned for.

"Yes" Chris replied "It seems that every now and then we get a ping. It happens when someone hits a rock that blows up."

"Like the one Zig was talking about?" The Captain was trying to put a frame around what was going on to see if Chris was on to something.

"Yes Sir. I have been watching for a couple hours now sir I am sure of it. There it happened again." Chris pointed at the screen. The scan that checks everything pinged.

"What does that scan check for?" Cheese asked the ensign. Honestly Chris didn't know so he just started talking looking at Spu with the hope he would jump in and save him.

"Well, it scans for everything. Energy of ships comms weapons fired everything." Chris didn't have a clue if he was right, he was just talking.

"It could just be weapons fire?" Cheese asked.

"No sir I have that turned off all weapons and engine filters on the scanner. It's something else."

"Spu open all comms to the idiots" Cheese ordered

"You mean the crew sir, right?" Spu didn't know what to make of the captain's comment.

"Yes, that's what I said?" Cheese told Spu back

"You called them idiots, Sir" Spu answered

"I said that out loud?" Cheese asked. I might be slowly losing my mind with all the bullshit I have to put up with on this ship he thought to himself. Spu turned back to look at his captain to see if he was ok. Cheese played it off like nothing happened.

"This is your captain speaking. I need everyone to cease on my order. 3…....2…....1…... cease fire. Ensign Chris has everyone stopped?" The captain asked. To his shock they had. Zig was the first to ask what was going on.

"What's the deal Cheese?" Zig and Cheese always talked as friends not as captain and crew. The captain did talk with all the crew like friends but jumped back and forth depending on the situation.

"Zig, something is going on remember the rocks you said blew up after you shot them. They seem to be sending out a signal." Cheese was happy Zig was the first to talk he could get right to the point. "Have you heard of anything like that before?"

"How do you know that it's happening every time?" Zig asked

"Chris spotted it" Cheese looked at Chris when he was speaking as if to say good job.

"It's Chris" Zig answered "He's wrong" Zig didn't trust Chris had any idea he knew what was going on and had no problem calling him out on it.

Cheese said "He has been checking and double checking he is right Zig." Zig wanted to know for sure.

"How many times did he double check" He asked

"He double checked it for the past 2 hours" Cheese had full confidence that Chris was right. He trusted his crew even the stupid ones. He knew that Chris wouldn't say anything if he didn't know he was right. Ensign Chris might even have known a full hour ago but he was checking and rechecking not to be wrong and look stupid Infront of the crew.

"Chris is right." Zig replied back to Cheese.

"Chris is right." The captain repeated looking at Chris when saying it. The smile Chris gave off was brighter that a sun. He was so proud. He looked over at Spu who gave his boy a fist bump as they both turned back down to the screens.

"Any idea's, Zig" The captain asked making sure to add Ziggy's name at the end so the whole crew didn't jump in.

"I don't know of anything you should open it up to the crew. With everything they have seen someone will know" It was a good idea.

"What have you got guys?" The captain asked. Moose was the first to answer.

"Its demon eggs and they are calling out to their mother. She is coming to eat us all. Hahaha." Moose was laughing about his idea Double H added.

"They are not eggs but summoning stones binding a super demon in place." Moose stop laughing and told Double H

"I can see that I have to try to make some sense." Cheese thought remembering why he didn't open things up to the crew it always turned out like this. He cut them both off.

"Say its not a demon portal to the under realm, any normal ideas?" JJB was trying to be one of the guys so he added his scary idea.

"It's a distress signal to the Vancar who are all going to port in and kill us." Spu asked the captain.

"Why don't we just ask Panda's friend?" Cheese answered.

"Good point. Panda what's the word can you call him?"

"Na still not talking to him and its too small a thing anyway. "Panda Answered.

"Good point it might be something small best not use one of our 3 wishes." Cheese could work this out he was sure of it.

"We don't get wishes." Panda told his captain

"I know that" Cheese replied "But you get what I mean. Any other ideas?" Cheese had run out and needed a bit of help and just like old times Zig did just that.

"Did you ask Arthune?" he said.

"Wouldn't he be on the ships open comms?" Cheese wanted to know?

"No, he turned his off a long time ago." Arthune always deemed himself more important that everyone else and if not him, the work he was doing was he didn't want to be bothered with the chatter of mortals, is the way he would put it.

"Spu, can you get him on comms?" Cheese needed to spend a little more time seeing what his crew was up to so some things like Arthune not being on the ship comms with everyone was not a surprise.

He was sure he would find things going on he would not be happy with and that could put the ship in real danger. But he would save that for another day.

"Sir, I have Arthune."

"Arthune this is your Captain speaking." Arthune clearly knew this but it was Cheese getting in the first shoot. One of many to come.

"What do you want, I am busy." Arthune barked back as if to say you are not my captain. Which is the way Arthune saw it.

"We have a reading and no one knows what it is."

"It's the coffee maker turn it off wait 10 sec and turn it on again." Normal Arthune looking down on everyone.

"No Arthune listen" Zig said and went on to tell him what was going on adding all the detail he could.

"Send me the data Chris" Arthune asked.

"Done you should have it." Chris was ahead of the game for once. Happy that he could do something right and wasn't a fuck up.

"Ok give me a sec to look at it" As Arthune was taking his time looking over the data every one of the crew was quiet. This was not a normal thing and it made the captain a bit uneasy. Thankfully it was not long before Arthune came back to everyone with an answer.

"It sends a signal all right. The signal goes out in all directions but that's just cover. They used to make them like this so you could hide a signal being sent to a hidden location. It was more a sales point than something that worked. I have sent the area in the asteroid field it's sending the signal to so everyone can see."

"Thanks Arthune let me take a look. On screen Spu." the captain ordered. "So its sending a signal to that big asteroid in the middle of a couple smaller ones then?" The captain talked out loud so the crew and Arthune would hear in the hope Arthune would give him more detail. Which he did.

"That's no asteroid that's a space station" Arthune answered

"It's too big to be a space station!" Cheese quickly said.

"It's not too big? Sir" Spu pointed out. The fleet had space station, so big you could fit a planet inside them. This was not a big space station. The captain just as quickly corrected himself.

"I meant to say it's too small to be a space station." That made a lot more sense. If you are going to build a space station you build it. Not some small thing only 30 ships could fit in. In a commercial station with that low a number of ships able to dock you wouldn't ever make the money back needed to keep it running. You always go big. So what was this?

"You are right Cheese people don't normally make them this small. But with all the pirates now there is a market for it." Arthune pointed out he didn't call the captain, captain. This was not something that crossed the Captains mind. The number of ship captains over the years that left Fleet, stealing the ship with the crew going along with it was a very big problem. The problem had got to the point where Fleet had made special units just to hunt down the deserters. The deserters did what they could to survive but it would seem most were just pirates. Raiding Fleet supple ships and anything else they could get their hands on was normal practice. With this many new pirates in space, companies had started making products to sell to them. Space stations to hide in was on that list. It was a very unknown, area but Arthune knew all about it. He might have even made the plans for base defense and a lot more for some of these companies under the table of course.

"The three smaller asteroids are base defense the small rocks are an early warning system and fail-safe system. If one is blown up or any signals are sent to the main base from them you can use the fail-safe system inside the asteroid that shuts down everything." Arthune was going into more details, he somehow knew. "What does the rest of the data look like?" Arthune wanted to see what else had been going on.

"What data?" Chris replied praying he didn't mess up after feeling great about the work he did to find this in the first place.

"The rest of the basic data on the scan I set up to always be running." Arthune already knew this was it the rest had been lost and he didn't need the answer. Pushing the idiot was mean after that.

"I filtered the other data noise out to make sure I was right and the signal wasn't a weapon or engine" Chris was justifying the reason to the rest of the crew not so Arthune would think differently of him. He needed the crew to know he had done his best and turning of the filters was the right thing to do to find out.

"It's not that you tunned them off its where you did it. You can just filter them on your screen, you know the thing you watch with the dots on. You turned them off on the master file. Now we don't know if any ships took off from the asteroid base or not. I supposes You could call them and ask them I guess?" Arthune did like to go with the mean option if he had the chance "Hey pirates would you like to give up or we will blast your very expensive rock!" Cheese cut in.

"It's not a bad idea. It does sound like something we would do. All up for knocking on the pirate's door and seeing if they want to come out and play say, YES SIR." The whole crew shouted

"Yes Sir." with that Arthune jump off the comms but not without saying.

"Love this ship but you guys are going to get us all killed. I am out." The next thing that was said was Moose yelling

"Space pirates! Come get some." The captain stopped the talk with some simple facts.

"We are on the way to training for us to stop and fight we would need to contact Fleet and get the go ahead." Spu turned back to Cheese and simply said to him.

"Then do it. It might get us out of this war mess." The captain didn't need to think about it any longer and gave Spu an order.

"Spu contact Fleet with a level 2 message stating our coordinates and that we stopped by to get firing practice at an asteroid field as we were days ahead of the meeting date for the training exercise. In doing so we have come across a pirate base and request orders. Let wait and see crew. Zig get your squadron back in the hanger and ready for anything that might happen. As for the rest of you stand down. Eat, sleep if you need to but be ready if we have to fight. This could get very real very fast." And with that the crew waited to hear back from Fleet about what to do next. Just after the captain finished talking.

"Space Pirates!!" was yelled by Moose one more time.

Chapter 9

Space pirates?

The crew were all waiting to hear if they can play hunt the pirates. With the full fire power of the S.S. No-Where and the skill of Divine squadron pirates don't stand much of a chance. It almost like shooting fish in a barrel. It didn't take long for Fleet to get back to them with an answer. To everyone's surprise. The answer was hunt the pirates. The captain addressed the crew.

"Fleet have answered our call and said we can hunt the pirates in this sector. They added a couple of extra points. We must have the ships monitor live feed sent to them and the second is, the pirate in the area is pirate Shoe, they want him dead or alive.

The crew were all back on comms and the first question was by Moose.

"Why do they want the ships monitor on live feed?"

"That way we can't lie to Fleet saying we need to check hull integrity and miss going to the front line. They can see no one hit us and call us out if we try and claim they did."

"Smart" Moose said seeming a little disappointed, that would have been a good way to get out of going to war. As Moose was talking, he carried on into the subjected about pirate Shoe.

"What's the deal with Sock bandit?" Moose wasn't going to use a stupid name like pirate shoe. If he needed to say a stupid name, he was going to make it up. So, sock bandit it was.

"There are a lot of details in the file you can read up on him in your own time." Captain Cheese wanted the crew to focused and not on some crazy story.

"He killed his kids in front of their mother and went mad." Spu told the whole crew.

"And this is going to happen now." Cheese said half under his breath knowing the crew would want the whole story. Which was a problem. The real details of what happened are all over the place. Yes, they know he killed his kids, and in front of his wife because it's on camera everything else might be real or could be story's no one really knows. It would turn out Shoe the pirate lied about everything so keeping something straight was nearly imposable. Who would think a pirate would lie! With Spu telling the crew the details they would want to know everything. This might take a while the captain thought to himself.

"Why the fuck would someone kill their own kids?" Moose asked. The crew was about to do what they normally did in totally horrifying situations. Make fun of everything so they didn't have to deal with the horror of the real world. It's the best way to cope.

"What if the kid was a total ass hat like you?" Double H asked Moose.

"Fair" is the only word Moose replied.

"What happened to his wife?" JJB asked

"No shock that's what you are thinking about" Alpha pulled him up about thinking of girls all the time.

"What do you mean? I care about women." JJB had to respond but it held no weight.

"The story goes he kept his wife to let the crew rape her" Spu told them

"Ok that's fucked up" Moose said.

"Killing the kids is ok and that's fucked up?" Double H asked Moose.

"Captain can we just go get this guy?" Moose was done listening to the stories and now wanted to get this guy.

"Yes, Moose we can. Can I get everyone on the same page now?" The captain didn't get much of an answer from anyone. "I need a yes sir from everyone." He said in a very strong voice.

"Yes sir." Came from the crew. They were slowly getting better at listening which was a surprise.

"I think the best way is to ask if they want to come out and play! Can you find the channel Spu?" Captain Cheese was going with the normal S.S. No-Where play. Do something stupid and see what happens.

"I found it." Spu replied.

"To the pirate Shoe surrender to the Imperial Fleet ship the S.S. No-Where and your crew can go free its only you we want." Cheese gave Spu the cut comms and then addressed the crew again. "What do we all think?"

"After thinking about it I call bullshit on Fleet wanting this guy for killing his kids why would Fleet care so much." Moose pointed out.

"Well, he did murder an Admiral and 20 offices one was his dad a war hero" Spu told Moose.

"Holy fuck why didn't you start with that?" Moose asked

"Its just the start, this guy is a piece of work." Spu told Moose.

"Yes, he is a shit can we stay on point of Operation Front Door." Cheese had a new great name for the mission.

"That's a great name, Sir." Chris told the captain.

"Captain we have a response." Spu notified Cheese.

"On screen Spu." Cheese liked playing captain. Even though he was he didn't often get the chance to act like it and say captaincy words. Spu put the message on screen. It was pirate Shoe himself. He didn't look like his picture in the Fleet profile. His hair was uncut and he had a straggly beard. Maybe he was going for the homeless pirate look Cheese thought to himself. If he was, he was doing a good job or maybe that's just what pirates looked like now. The No-Where didn't really fight them if at all so this might be a first for Cheese.

"Pirate Shoe for crimes against The Imperial Fleet and just about everyone else we can think of we have been ordered to bring you in dead or alive. If you give yourself up your crew can pass, Fleet has no fight with any of them." Cheese delivered the mandate with authority sounding like a true captain of the fleet. Boring. There was no way Shoe would give up, on that 'I wouldn't'. Cheese told himself.

"It's pirate LORD shoe." Shoe made a point of saying. "They sent the S.S. No-Where after me hey? I didn't think your crew would turn pirate hunter as you act more like pirates than part of Fleet anyway."

"We didn't get sent after you Shoe" Cheese decided to act more like himself not like a by the book Fleet captain. He might get what was needed faster and if he didn't, he wouldn't pretend to be someone he was not.

"Again, pirate LORD" Shoe corrected the captain a second time. "Looks like they did why else would you shoot every asteroid in the sector?" Shoe made a very good point and the captain was not about to try and explain the stupid game the ship and the crew where playing. It would be laughable at best and would make him look like a complete idiot. Cheese thought it would be smart to not act like he had said anything.

"So are we coming to get ya? The crew kind of wants a fight. You have 5 minutes to answer think among yourselves and give us an answer." Cheese gave the order to cut comms again to Spu which he did. "Crew I want a boarding team to meet me in the hanger now, anyone who wants to fight meet me at the shuttle. Divine squad you follow us in giving us cover. The three defensive towers on the outside need to disappear.

"I have already done one" JJB's voice came over the comm's. The captain was in the ships transport system heading to the shuttle bay with his personal comms.

"Not following orders again Jig." Cheese was happy he didn't it would make things faster.

"Remember this is a boarding team to take a pirate space station if you don't have the fight for it don't come. If you do bring big guns."

"Captain are you not going to wait for an answer? Maybe the crew is going to give themselves up?" Chris didn't understand why he wouldn't wait.

"Would anyone of you turn me in to save your life?" The captain answered

"WELL!" Moose was about to say yes but started laughing

"I see your point SIR." Chris replied

"This way we get a head start" As the captain finished his words the door opened to the shuttle bay. The ship seemed to move faster when the crew needed it to. Then the captain remembered the stoner AI that runs it and called out to him.

"Gary, you got the ship until I get back shoot anything that is not us. Unless we say not to ok." The captain was now on the shuttle and everyone from the crew was already there waiting on him.

"Let's go" Ordered the captain, as the doors closed two more crew jumped on. It was Spu and Chris. The ship was out of the hangar in space and moving to the target before the captain noticed and then he lost it.

"What the hell are you two doing here? Who is running the ship what makes you come up with the ideas you have! What!" The captain's face was red so Spu told him.

"You said anyone could come it's on you." Spu was not taking any blame, he wanted to steal from pirates.

"I followed what Spu said Sir. You know stealing from pirates and all." Spu hit Chris, he wasn't meant to say the real reason to the captain. Chris put his arms out and shrugged his shoulders like he was supposed to know better. He didn't. He saw Cooper sitting on the side and nodded his head to say hi like to old friends might do. The captain didn't calm down with Spu's answer.

"I will deal with both of you later!" Cheese realized there was not point wasting energy on it now. The shuttle had taken off. To go back would waste time.

"I don't understand Sir we have the drop on them with the whole "we will call you back in 5 minutes"" Spu was trying to justify his bad actions

"No Spu you total idiot" Cheese was in a bad mood and wasn't going to hold back. "We had the time if you two kept him on hold. Its 7 minutes to fly to the asteroid plus the time to get to the ship. This only helps him to be ready. After he cut you two idiots off, he would know the flight time and use that as a guide. Now he will just be waiting for us." The captain looked hard at Spu and Chris if anyone died or anything went wrong the captain would hold them responsible. Spu swallowed hard. Chris didn't notice. This changed the mood in the shuttle for some people but not for Moose.

"Idiots there is a reason we don't let you off the bridge" he said taunting them. "Captain they are staying on the shuttle, right?" Moose asked not waiting to deal with them in combat.

"I think that's for the best they will get in the way in combat. Do you two understand that? Stay on the shuttle! I will say it one more time. STAY IN THE SHUTTLE!" Cheese looks at Moose and said softly "That should do it." Moose did a giggly smile at Cheese. It was like the parents just told off the kids and for some reason are happy about it. Rush and Panda were both up front flying the shuttle Rush turned back to inform the captain all three of the outer defense turrets were destroyed and they have a clean run at the main asteroid. The asteroid base defense guns are not going to slow the heavy combat shuttle down. As they were only a couple of minutes out from landing some of the crew looked up with a bit of concern as they could hear the gun fire hitting the outer hull. The old heads like Moose and double H don't seem to even notice. The ship entered the docking bay which was very large and empty. It landed as far up as it could to the door which looked like it entered the rest of the base. The combat shuttle had ramps you could deploy from the front and the back. The one at the front was under the cockpit one level down. This was a good way to exit the ship because the main guns could support you as you moved out of the ship and at the same time keep you safe in the firing arc.

      The fire team hit the ground with Moose and Double H at the front like normal. Cooper was following closely behind with no real clue of what was going on, it seems some fool gave him a gun. They headed for the large door off to the right-hand side of the bay. As soon as they moved out of the safety of the ships firing arc they came under fire from the pirates.

"Contact" Moose Shouted as a hail of gun fire rained down on the front men. From behind Moose and Double H the cover fire came from the ship. Panda killing two with the first shots. With the two bodies hitting the floor gun fire from the pirates stopped. Moose popped his head out from his cover spot to get a better look.

"They are heading for the door." He called on comms.

"Numbers?" Panda asked

"10-14 I think" Moose replied. Panda put 14 marks on his left arm and then crossed 2 out.

"Moving." Moose called, both he and Double H slowly started to move forward. Checking every corner as not to be flanked. When they reached the door, the pirates had ran through they stopped and called back.

"Clear." Moose looked back towards the ship seeing Cheese coming towards him with Rush and Panda. He asked the captain. "What's the plan?"

"It's clearly a trap. They want us to follow them into some death shoot out area they have planned." Cheese answered, not looking like he had an idea.

"Sir" Spu came over the Comms "There is another door on the left side of the hangar it ends up in the same place but from a different side. It might be the play." Cheese turns to the 4 guys and say's,

"Hey I think there is a door on the left side of the hangar let's try that." It wasn't like the rest of the crew hadn't heard Spu speak but they let the captain have this one. On the walk across the hangar 6 other ships were in the bays. They found Cooper on the way just walking around like nothing was going on. Rush opened the door with ease the system didn't seem to have any extra security. As the crew walked in one by one, they heard a beep as Cooper walked past the door. Everyone stopped, looked back but nothing seemed to happen or be out of place. The beep might have sounded a trap. Something might blow up or it could just be the door beeped. Walking into a pirate base it could be anything. The group then did one extra check, looking and looking at each other as if to ask did you see anything? After a couple of shoulder shrugs and raised eyebrows, everything seemed ok so the group moved forward. The corridors seemed like any other corridors of a star ship. Moose was at the head of the group trying to push forward as fast as he could.

"I think we should go to the left captain." Moose was making a call about which way they should head at the cross roads in which they found themselves in front of.

"Why do you think that Moose" The captain asked not really having a good idea which way to go. So he was very happy to hear input from Moose.

"We left the hangar on the left sided door if we keep going left that should put the inner part of the ship on our right. This way that's the only side we can get jumped from." Moose explained the reason and it seemed to make sense to everyone.

"To the left." Cheese said looking at Moose who returned the words.

"To the left." The crew moved forward now on the same page knowing the goal was to work their way to the commend center of the pirate asteroid. Keeping the enemy to the right-hand side. The crew took the next two left turns at the cross roads without enemy contact. They stopped to check every door along the way. It seemed this part of the ship was engineering and storage. Nothing of interest was found. With all the checking and walking the crew had been out for a couple of hours without finding anything. Moose stopped the group and asked.

"Do you hear that?" He was pointing down the hallway down which they were heading. The crew froze hit the sides of the corridors, unlike normal in combat the crew were the best they could be a force people feared working around a rat maze didn't fit their skill set. The main problem was keeping them in that mind set. Cooper was not a normal member of the crew and was pushed to the side by Cheese. After an evil look at Cooper Cheese put his attention down the Hall at the noises waiting to fire. A familiar voice was heard.

"Hey, Captain its us!" The voice shouted from around the corner.

"It's us don't shoot." a different voice said. Two people slowly came into view. It was Spu and Chris. Moose started to laugh.

"I told you both to stay on the SHIP!" the captain yelled at them.

"But sir." Spu tried to tell the captain why he came off the shuttle but Cheese seemed too mad. Spu thought it was best for him to burn himself out yelling first.

"Don't you but SIR ME!" the captain started in on Spu. He didn't look at Chris because he knew that he just followed whatever Spu said. "I told you to stay on the Shuttle and you couldn't even do that what else are you going to fuck up on this mission!" Spit was flying out of Cheese's mouth bouncing off Spu's face. Then the captain stopped. He was looking at Spu and noticed that Spu look. He wasn't trying to hold back? He had that Spu look on his face. The Spu look was a mix of I am right and you don't know what I know. It was more than a smug git look. It was a knowing smug not just smug git. A knowing of I am about to make you look a fool and the captain spotted this. "Anything you want to tell me Spu?" The captain asked.

"I could help you with the reason you can't find the pirates." Spu answered with clearly more to say on the matter. He was going to make the captain ask him to help. Cheese wasn't going to waste time or try and find a trick to catch Spu into telling him.

"Out with it Spu what do you know." The captain seemed to cut out that anger he had for Spu not following orders but he was still red faced from the yelling.

"As you know we don't have a map of inside this asteroid base. But you all do have your trackers on. Watching your trackers, you can see you have been walking in circles. Well, it's more of a figure of 8. You are about to make your fourth run down the same corridor so I came to tell you." Spu finished explaining to the captain. He had a smile on his face so big it looked like it was glowing. He couldn't wait to hear the Captain say sorry for yelling at him in front of the crew and that he was right to disobey orders. The captain turned to the rest of the boarding party and said.

"It looks like we made a wrong turn at this first cross roads. Let double back to that point maybe we can find a way around them." The captain and the boarding party start to head back the way Spu and Chris just came from. Walking behind everyone the smile on Spu's face had completely gone. Captain Cheese was not going to say anything about the clear fuck up. He might say well done to Spu later back on the ship but never in front of the crew. It would send the message that everyone could question him and that was not a good way to be a Captain. It's a good way for someone else to take over the ship. Cheese made a point of walking slower back to the cross roads double checking the few doors along the way. He was not going to make a second mistake on this mission. The trust of a crew can break over time, a smart captain doesn't let the cracks set in stopping problems before they start. They reached the crossroads.

"Ok let's head down this way. We know we are walking into the pirates this way so let's get on point, no slip ups. Spu Chris, I want you both at the back." After Cheese finished speaking, he gave

Spu a death look. Spu dropped in line in fear the captain might just shoot him for showing him up.

"Yes Sir." Spu acknowledged the captain back with a head nod, as if to say I am sorry for the way i pointed out the problem. He grabbed Chris and headed to the back covering the rear of the away team. Moose was back at the front with Double H like normal. Cooper was not with them but at a second line with the captain with Panda and rush covering everyone.

"This is going to be a mess Cheese!" Moose yelled putting a little extra volume in his voice. "They have had a lot more time to set if we were walking into a trap before now

"It's a double trap." Double H finished the sentence. The front two both looked at everyone knowing all hell could break lose at any time. They pushed forward into a big open room with crates stacked in the mid and sides. There were no reason for the crates to be stacked in this way. Moose understood this was set for an ambush. He raised his hand to stop the party. He whispered into the comms

"Its an ambush, Panda we will push them to you." Moose and double H moved into the room pushing down one side, scanning on the way round so not to get caught by a radio or trip mine. Keeping their backs to the wall they made short work clearing the room and getting back to the party.

"The room is all clear Sir. We found a couple new toys, other than that nothing here. We are clear to move" Moose said to Cheese. Calling the captain Sir was something he used to do in the old ground wars him and the captain fought together. It was a habit he slipped into when in combat situations. Away from the brash loud talking back to the Captain, Moose was back into the professional killer Moose.

"You said ambush?" Cheese said Moose knowing he doesn't get things like this wrong.

"It was set, I think they moved back deeper into the asteroid after the time we gave them walking about they must have moved back to set up. Its going to be tuff ahead." Moose answered.

"We are moving on." Cheese called over the Comms. The team started off one more time trying to find this pirate group. Cheese was not looking forward to the fight ahead, he didn't want to lose a member of the crew. One wild card was the new guy, Cooper. The crew didn't know how this guy could fight. It seemed most of the crew didn't trust him 100% yet, but that didn't matter if he was good with a gun. The captain looked over at Cooper to see how he was doing with the stress of the mission. To the captain's surprise Cooper was smiling and looked like he didn't have a care in the world! Then the captain noticed that Cooper wasn't carrying a weapon.

"Cooper why don't you have a weapon?" the Captain asked.

A noise came over the comms. It was two beeps. It was a signal from Moose to look at him. The captain turned to look at the front of the away team seeing Moose looking back at him. He was just shaking his head to the captain as if to say NO. His eyes told the rest of the story to Cheese. Cheese nodded back as to say I understand. Which he clearly didn't and it was something he would have to get back to Moose on later. This story was going to be good. It had to be to not have one extra gun in the fight.

    The team moved past the massive crate room and into another section of the ship. This was clearly the living area. A big open rec room with a kitchen down one end screens everywhere and a game you played with sticks in the middle. Off to the other side away from the kitchen looked like the pirate's quarters. It could be filled with all kinds of stuff or maybe just killer pirates!

Moose and Double H started down the first corridor that led into the quarters looking for contact with the pirates. After a very small amount of time, they were back in the rec room with the rest of the team. The team were giving the rec room a going over looking for anything of use.

"Nothing captain." Moose said on the comms quietly "the rooms have been looted and they are gone. I will check the other two quarter runs but I think its going to be the same." A quarter run was nothing more than a corridor with quarters on both sides. The only difference being they are set up by rank. You have all the same rank people down one corridor. Its not done on fleet ships but out in the private sector its very normal. Moose and Double H rejoined the team with everyone ready to push through a big door in the middle of the rec room behind the table with the stick game on it when Spu's voice picked up.

"What if Chris and I cover here and follow back to you guys in 5 mins sir? That way no one can come in behind." This was very normal combat maneuvers but for Spu to volunteer didn't seem right. Maybe he was trying to make up for calling out the captain in front of the crew. It didn't matter Cheese needed someone to do this and it might as well be them.

"Ok Spu, you and Chris cover the rear, the rest of us push on. And Spu don't fuck this up." The captain added at the end. Knowing full well Spu could just fall asleep on the job. Spu did seem to have it under control. He grabbed Chris and moved away as everyone else went through the large door in the middle of the rec room. With no contact yet Moose and Double H started to get on edge as this large corridor only had one door at the end. The pirates had to be in the area past that door. They had been everywhere else on the asteroid base. After the door opens, all hell was going to break lose. In this corridor there was no place to hide. All the others had something. A little cover to get behind not here, they would be sitting ducks. Very smart of the pirates to make this the spot for a battle. If they came in behind at the same time, the crew would not have a chance. A feeling of dread started to set in over everyone. No words were needed everyone's eyes told a story wide open and focused. Head nods were going around the crew like a wave to get ready for the moment the doors opened. Panda and Rush had the back and front covered with everyone else looking at the door. Moose was going to smash open the door. He was always the front man. Luck was on his side to never get shot. One last breath as heart rates slowed weapons ready. Then suddenly the door open! Cooper had opened it and walked in like he was on a stroll in the park with the wind blowing taking his dog for a walk.

"Cooper!!" Cheese shouted "Get back here." The Captain was sure like everyone else watching he was going to see Cooper be shot so many times there would be nothing left of him. But Cooper didn't hear him and just kept walking into the room that looked like the bridge.

"Cooper get back here!" Cheese yelled one more time but louder. This time he did hear. He stopped walking and slowly turned around to look at the crew. At this point Moose was full hand on head waiting for him to be totally blown away. Cooper just looked back with anger on his face.

"What!" Cooper yelled

"Get back here." The captain was not yelling this time but mostly speaking under his breath so not to make too much noise. Which was mute at this point.

"I figured everyone was scared to walk in the room so I did." Cooper said with a shrug of his shoulders not seeing the big deal. "what's the big deal?" He asked everyone. "No one is here."

"You don't know that." Double H pointed out. Cooper looked at Double H with a funny looked then yelled as loud as he could

"Is anyone here!?" It was deadly quiet but even Moose looked up to see if anyone answered. Which of course they didn't because it seemed no one was left on the asteroid. Moose started to laugh. Cooper just turned and walked off to sit in the captain's chair. Everyone was completely shocked by the total stupidity of Coopers actions. Panda and Rush didn't move. Moose and double H looked around the bridge looking into every corner to see if this was really happening. Cheese walked in wondering at the stupidly of Cooper and hoped they were not waiting to just shot him. He did however have bigger things on his mind. If he had cleared the base and found no pirates, where were they hiding? did they get off? They fought them in the hangar? Things were not adding up and he needed to think. How much time did that walk around the engineering bay cost them? What did the pirates do? How many more traps had they set for them? Moose was soon to have some answers.

"I have checked both rooms on two of the sides Cheese. One is the captains' quarters it has nothing in it. The other is a briefing room no traps no explosives nothing, all clear." Moose told Cheese.

"This doesn't add up yet. We are missing something." Cheese was saying we but meaning him.

 "We are missing the pirates." Cooper added. Cheese walk over and asked him to get out of the captain's chair. Cooper did ask if he could be the captain, Cheese simply patted him on the head and sat down. It wasn't his chair but it would help him think. He started to think out loud.

"They can't have just left their base, their home." Cheese said out loud. Normally his number two would answer but he didn't Cheese look towards him. Then he noticed. Dan his second, his first officer, was not with them they left him on the ship. Cheese asked everyone in a panic.

"Where is Office Feet?" Getting his name wrong in the panic.

"I like office Feet." Cooper replied. Cheese was starting to think the Cooper was a small child who somehow got out of day care. A very stupid small child and then for some reason they gave him a gun and let him lose in the universe. Something would have to been done about him but now was not the time.

Moose however started to laugh

"Did we forget him?" He answered inquisitively to Cheese with a bundle of laughter. No one trusted Feet and no one cared he wasn't with them. Cheese again started to think out loud.

"What if Feet's plan was to steel the NoWhere to get back to his girl? Na Gary would stop him."

"Didn't you lock Gary out of the bridge Sir?" Panda pointed out a very important fact to the captain. This didn't look good.

"He can't fly the ship. Arthune is still on board with Harry everything is fine." Double H stepped back in to settle the captain down.

"Yea its not like the ship is going to be taken over by pirates when we are away!" Moose said to Cheese laughing and chuckling to himself.

He might have worked out what was really going on. The Captains Brain started to flood with ways and idea how the pirates could pull something like taking the No-Where off. If they watch Spu and Chris land and flew right after, the main group of pirates could just fly away to the NoWhere and take her. This would get them out of going to war. The Captain joked with himself but this is a real problem. Captain Cheese understood that this was a real emergency and needed to contact Arthune as he didn't and couldn't trust Feet. Saying to himself in his head 'can't think of an emergency like this one.' Buzz Buzz Buzz Buzz.

"What the hell is that noise!" The captain yelled to the top of his voice. At that moment the door to the bridge had two more layers clamp down extra blast doors. With the doors sealed the Buzzing stopped and the lights on the ship went from a clear white to a menacing red glow. The main view screen started to turn on slowly, Cheese looked at Cooper and yelled.

"What the hell did you just do!!"

Cooper looked back at him and said

"But you said emergency, so I hit the button that said emergency."

Cheese started to think to himself, did he say that out loud he was sure he didn't and kept that in his head. Could Cooper read his mind? What was he thinking he could just ask Moose?

"Moose, did I say that out loud?" The captain asked but before Moose could answer the main screen had booted up and a message had started to play.

Chapter 10
New Friends

The crew on the bridge of the pirate asteroid base watched as the main view screen came online. After being cut off from the rest of the away team, this made everyone a little nervous. It was a good tactic to pick the crew apart, spread them out, and kill them off. No one could hear gun fire back in the rec room yet maybe the message on the screen would hold some answers. A very dirty looking pirate came on to the screen. He had a patchy beard with greasy brown hair. If you were to think of a dirty pirate this is what you would think of, it was the pirate Shoe. The message started.

"I see you found your way into my control room and like fools locked yourself in. By now you must have found out that the doors cannot be opened from there. It's a safety feature to stop people stealing our base while we are away stealing. You should think about one for your ship." There was a pause in Shoe's speech this gave time for Cheese to understand that he was going after the NoWhere!

"After we take your ship any of the crew that doesn't join us will be killed. On the pay you give them it's not going to be hard to get them to fight for me. Then we will be back for you." And with that the screen cut off.

"Jokes on him we don't have a crew." Moose said laughing the whole time.

"Before we start thinking about the NoWhere let's see if he is telling the truth can we open the doors on this piece of crap." Cheese was not going to let some pirate take his ship.

"We can get out of this anytime. Call your friend Panda." Moose asked full of confidence.

"NOPE, we are still not talking. Anyway he wouldn't help. He would laugh and say it's our own fault for getting in this mess." Panda answered.

"You are still not talking!" Moose was shocked to hear this. "How long has it been?"

"Couple months, I think but he always comes back." Panda seemed confident he wouldn't help. Moose didn't push the issue. He believed him as Panda was always true to his word and on the up and up.

"Can we please CHECK if the doors can be opened!" Cheese yelled. He didn't think Panda and Moose's conversation was worth having, they need to fix this problem themselves. He looked over just in time to see Cooper slap the big button again. A buzzer went off again with a big crash as a third wave of drops hit closed on the main door.

"STOP HITTING THAT BUTTON!" Cheese yelled at Cooper.

"I was thinking as it closed the door maybe it could open it." Which did seem like a valid way to approach the situation. It wasn't completely stupid. Who was to know it would add a third layer on the door?

"YOU DON'T TOUCH ANYTHING!" The captain's eyes looked like they had turned red with blood, his hands had been bawled into fists out of stress, no, it was because he wanted to punch Cooper! "Strap him up and tie him down in a chair. Now!" The captain ordered. Not having a clue on how to deal with Cooper who looked at him and said.

"But you're the one that moved me out of the chair." Cheese lost it.

"Sit your ASS IN THAT CHAIR AND DON'T MOVE OR I'LL SHOOT YOU!" With all the yelling the captains voice cracked the rest of the crew just stared at their leader who they had never seen lose his cool. They had been with him for years in combat, real warzones. They couldn't even remember him raising his voice. He might just shoot this Cooper guy. Moose didn't even laugh he just had his eyes wide open, shocked at what was happening. Then everyone's eyes started to move over to Cooper who was walking as if the captain was going to shoot him. He looked so scared going to sit in the captain's chair which Cheese had moved well away from. It wasn't completely understood if Cooper knew what was going on. Did this all happen because Cheese asked him to move from the chair? Maybe next time the course of action was not to act. As Cooper sat down you couldn't help but feel sorry for the little guy. He was about in tears. The crew did one of the things they did best. Act like nothing has happened and just carry on. Double H was looking at the computers then looked up.

"It seems that the computers power down when that message comes on screen. The message is set to run at the same time so you don't notice. The only time you had to stop it happening you were watching the screen. Simple and smart.

"Can you repower them?" Cheese asked

"No, they don't just power down they lock. I have a feeling that one of the panels back in the engineering area is the only place to restart it."

"Can we reach Spu to see if he can do the power reset?"

"The channels are blocked. I am working on a way around it now." Rush answered.

"Ok let Rush work on that. Can we use these systems to contact Arthune on the NoWhere or maybe Divine squad to see what's going on, on the outside?" The captain was just trying to find some way forward out of this mess. You could hear his nerviness in his voice.

"Everything is out" Double H stated "Everything with power is gone. We have the emergency lights and emergency air and that's it. If I play with the power to try and use that to restart everything it might cut the air off. We are going to find it very hard to breath in about 20 mins as we are just running on emergency air. So, we had better do something before then." Things like this were normal for the crew of the NoWhere. Big problems and little time everyone had their role and they played it very well. Moose's role was to shoot stuff nothing to shoot so he was out.

"I'm going to take a nap then," he said. No one blinked an eye at this because this was not a Moose and Panda problem. They both sat down out of the way. Sitting close to the point where the air came into the bridge. Cheese carried on down the list he had in his head to fix the situation.

"No coms, no power, what's stopping our coms getting out, and can we stop that?" He asked the two working on getting them out of this problem. Rush stepped in to point out what seemed to be happening.

"We can't send anything out, and nothing can come in by the looks of what I am seeing. H can you check this. Some field is around the bridge." Double H walked over to Rush to look at his personal scanner.

"If we can find any part of this, we can stop the shield blocking our comms and get a signal to the NoWhere or maybe to Spu."

"I don't know what you mean but get on it. Do we have anything else if this doesn't work?" The captain finished with.

"I don't think so." Rush answered as H looked into shutting the shield around the bridge down. The clock was ticking with the air running low. The air was not going to run out to the point they would die but it would get so low that everyone would lose consciousness. At that point the No-Where was lost. The pirates would walk back in to a room of unconsciousness people. There would be no big gun fight no going down in a blaze of glory they would all be helpless. All but Moose that is. With all the bio upgrades and implanted tec it's not known if he needs air to breath anymore. This was something they were going to find out if they can't get a signal out soon.

"I can't do it." Double told Cheese. "The shield is just too strong and I don't have the power to push through it."

"I can't shut the shield down that's blocking the comms." Rush also informed the captain.

"Let's switch." H told Rush

"Good idea maybe we missed something" Rush answered with a bit of hope. It was sometimes a good idea to switch what you are working on with someone. Maybe you missed something and the other person would find the answer. Maybe you would find the answer to the problem. Cheese looked on and checked his watch they had been at it for over 15 minutes already. Time was running short. It didn't seem that long. Time does have a funny way of speeding up when you don't need it to and torturing you by slowing down when you don't need it to. Cheese was going to make a point in asking God about that one the next time he talked to him. Cheese then turned to Moose and Panda.

"Ideas?" He asked.

"You run out of air and I kill everyone that comes in the door?" Moose said. Panda didn't answer he just had his eyes shut. He didn't move.

"Sounds like a plan." Cheese said.

"No luck again." Double H spoke out not finding a way out. He did however come up with a different idea." Maybe Spu is going to understand what's going on and get the power on?" He did mean it but everyone started to laugh at his idea.

"Spu is still trying to steal what he can, he is not going to notice anything." Cheese pointed out.

"But he did save us walking in circles." Double H pointed out which was a good point.

"That was only because he was looking for a reason to steal. That gave him his way to talking to us. I bet if I ask Chris spotted it and told Spu anyway." The captain pointed out. "Good try guys" Cheese said as he looked about. "The plan is Moose kills everyone who comes through the door. The rest of us find a place behind a console so we can't be seen when the door opens." And with that Cheese made his way behind a computer console to the left side of the door. Double H and Rush sat over on the right side where they were both working. As they all sat down a small beep beep beep went off. It was the timer the captain set for 20 minutes.

"That's 20 minutes boys have a good nap" With that the captain closed his eyes to just wait.

Chapter 11
The Escape Plan

It could have been a couple hours or even a couple of days that passed for the crew from the S.S. NoWhere who were waiting in the control room of the pirate asteroid base. Moose would have known how long they had been in there. As he didn't need air to breath like the rest of the crew, but he fell asleep. The last of the main doors to the control room opened and air filled the room. The 4-crew started to breath in the air and in a few minutes, they would be back to normal but with a massive headache. That's if the pirates didn't just shoot them first.

Double H was the first of everyone to fully awake. He stood up from the point he had been hiding and looked over at the door. He didn't have the energy to pull up his weapon he was in the mind set if he was going to be shot fuck it as his mind was not working correctly yet. When he looked at the door, he saw a familiar face.

"O hi!" He said then stretched his arms out feeling like he had awoken from a great night's sleep. With him speaking the words it seemed to help bring everyone else back around. Voices and no gun fire these were a good sign. The captain was the next to fully awake. He wasn't as fast to jump up on his feet. He kept his eyes closed so it didn't look like he was awake yet. He wanted to hear the voices, to see who opened the door and had got the air restarted. This would help him in which option to take next. He could hear Double H talking and laughing but he didn't recognize the other voice but it did sound familiar. It did seem to only be one person at the door. The captain's headache was pounding and his eyes were very blurry. He moved to his feet to look over the computer terminal to get a look at the person in the doorway. As he looked up, he could see a man standing solo in the door way. Cheese had his gun ready in his right hand to shoot at the first chance he got. But then he noticed.

"Feet?" The captain shouted. At the door was 1st LT Dan Feet. With a light coming in behind him lighting him up. This made him look very angelic. It was because the main lights in the control room hadn't come back on yet. None the less it made him look more or of a hero than maybe he was, Cheese thought to himself.

"Sir," Feet replied to the captain. With a cocky smile on his face.

"It's about time you got here." Cheese replied. He could feel his body ache as he was getting to his feet. He was no longer young and a couple of hours on a cold metal floor now takes a toll. He was going to play this off like it was all part of a plan. He planned all along for Feet to come and resecure them. This didn't mean the captain was going to start to trust him but it did move him up a bit in his mind. After all the captain has been ordered to dispose of Feet for whatever reason by the Lord Admiral Miku. He couldn't think of anything else the tracker would be used for. 1st officer Feet didn't bite on the captain's little comment.

"I can see you have everything under control here, Sir." Feet hit back with a sarcastic tone. Cheese did want to go back and for with Feet but he really wanted to know how his ship was.

"Is the ship, ok?" Cheese was going to put his cards on the table and get straight to the point. He didn't know the length of time he was out and needed to get to business.

"The Ship?" Feet answered "Why would the ship be in danger? And who is Gary?" This didn't help the captain piece anything together. The pirates clearly said they are going to try and take the No-Where. It seemed the ship's AI let Feet out, this needed to be addressed. The last thing the captain wanted was to talk about the fact they have AI on the ship. Everyone knows you don't have AI, because at some point it takes over the universe and kills everyone. History showed this over and over. First thing's first where are the pirates. Cheese told Feet about the message the pirates left. They both had puzzled looks on their faces.

"What was Spu and Chris up to?" Cheese asked as Feet must have walked past them on the way in. If they can't find the pirates maybe they can piece something else together about what was going on the captain was thinking.

"I didn't see them?" Feet replied.

"You should have? They are in the canteen area." The captain said as he started to walk to the door. He was going to find out what's going on.

"Looks like we are on the move." Panda said to Moose as they both reluctantly got up and followed. Double H was already by the captain's side. He was trying to get ahead of Cheese to give the guys a head's up that the captain was coming so they could stop whatever stupid thing Spu had got them into. As the first three, Feet, Cheese and Double H walked, the captain asked Feet.

"What made you fly to the asteroid?"

"No one answered me on comms. I spotted the base felt like it was the right play. I did talk to Divine Squadron on the flight over. They said you all landed here. So I came to help." Feet explained.

"As I planned." Cheese replied keeping his head facing forward not to look at Feet. Feet on the other hand turned to look at the captain with a face that said it all. Was the captain crazy. Double H was just smiling backing his captain over the new guy no matter how stupid the captains 'plan' sounds.

"Spu!" Double H called loudly taking the conversation onto something else. "Your captain needs you now!" This was clearly to give Spu a heads-up Cheese was coming and to get ready. Cheese gave Double-H a disapproving look. He wanted to catch Spu red handed. Which turns out wasn't hard. Spu and Chris both came out of the side quarters wearing all kinds of clothes.

"A…. What is going on with you two?" The captain asked. They both had layers and layers of clothes on. All different kinds of jackets, shirts you can think of, stacked on each other. They had chains around their necks and big gold rings. They even had extra trousers on. They must have been hot and found it very hard to move. The captain was shocked they could even walk with the number of clothes they had on.

"So……" Cheese said waiting for them to answer.

"It was Spu's idea." Chris said. The captain and Office Feet both turned and looked at Chris as if to say don't bullshit us. It was the look they had worked with each other for years and understood what the other was thinking. Which was, you are a grown man you can make up your own mind? Then turned back to Spu who everyone knew was really running the show. Spu was looking at Chris.

"Thanks Nerd!" Spu said. Not happy that Chris double crossed him.

"Spu?" The captain pulled Spu's attention back to him away from Chris's double cross.

"What? It's not like the pirates are going to need this stuff!" Spu's face was red with all the extra clothes on.

"Is this the reason you came to find us in the first place?" The captain was then thinking back to the way Spu jumped onto the Ship when clearly ordered to stay on the No-Where.

"NO" Spu answered in a way that clearly was a yes. "It's not like its stealing" He went on.

"How? How is this not stealing?" Office Feet barked at Spu. The captain was happy to see Fett had his back.

"Well, they stole it first, so now it's free because the first owners don't own it and the second owners are not here!" Spu answered looking proud, that he was right in his mind.

"You are still stealing from the second owners! You idiot! And how do you not know they didn't buy this crap in the first place!?!" Fett was in full flow. Cheese was happy not to be playing the bad guy. Spu was not going to stop just like normal.

"If we blow this place the stuff is going to burn in space so maybe we are keeping it safe until we see the pirates again." Spu seemed happy with himself over this answer so much so Chris spoke up.

"That's what we are doing, keeping it safe for the pirates." Then Spu put it back to the captain

"You are going to blow this place up, right?" The captain didn't want to deal with any of this. That's when Moose and Panda caught up with them. They could tell because as soon as Moose saw Spu and Chris he started to laugh.

"What the hell are you two idiots wearing!" He asked. This seemed like a good time to move on and deal with this later.

"We will deal with you two idiots later right now we need to get back the No-Where and see what happened to the pirates." Cheese walked off to the flight deck with everyone following. Spu and Chris were finding it hard to keep up. It was made harder with Moose stopping them to take the best rings off them. They couldn't stop him not just because of the bioimplants Moose had but they couldn't move their arms very well at all.

    As the away team reached the room Moose had cleared of explosives, he yelled for everyone to stop.

"STOP!" He yelled "Which door did you come in" He looked at office Feet.

"That one" Office Feet pointed to the same door they had all walked in.

"We go back that way" Moose told everyone

"But I am sure that ways faster" Spu said trying to get back to the shuttle as fast as he can. The weight of the cloths was starting to be a problem for him.

"Go ahead!" Moose said "Just wait until we are out of the room so we don't blow up with you" Moose was walking to the same door they came in.

"Do you think they set the door to blow?" Cheese calmly asked Moose.

"It's what I would do." Moose then went on to set the whole plan out. "When we walked in the wrong door and took all that time walking about, they set off. This was the place Shoe wanted to fight us when that didn't happen, they set a trap on the door and left. If some of us die great if not they could get us on the way out. Only an idiot would open that door." Moose said that last part looking at Spu.

"So I am the ship idiot Spu?" Spu asked not wanting anyone to answer. But double H did.

"Na that's Cooper, you have a long way to get that title back Spu." The captain put his hand to his head Cooper was not with them.

"We forgot Cooper back in the control room. God knows what he is doing." Cheese looked up at Panda.

"I will go back and get him. Sir" Fett told the captain. "We can fly back on the shuttle I came in not to slow you down." This lieutenant Dan Fett was starting to show his worth.

"Don't let him touch anything." Cheese told Fett. "I mean nothing Dan." He called me by my first name Fett thought to himself, as he jogged back to the control room. The captain was starting to warm to his first officer. Maybe this wasn't going to be complete hell until he could get off ship and back to his Catherine. Although he still needed to get off this base without Cooper doing something stupid first.

Office Fett got to the control room. He had to look around to find Cooper. When he did, he was sound asleep.

"Cooper wake up." Fett called "Cooper we need to go." Cooper slowly opened his eyes and pulled his hands out from under his head. He was using them as a pillow under his head. He had them together like he was praying. By the way he was laying down it must have hurt his hands. Fett noticed this.

"Doesn't that hurt your hands?" He asked Cooper. Cooper was in his own world.

"Is this a dream? You didn't come with us Sir." Cooper said.

"No this is not a dream Cooper." Fett had forgotten how stupid Cooper really was.

"The captain yelled at me for hitting a button. I was only trying to help everyone." Cooper told Fett. It was sad listening to him talk. It was like a beaten puppy trying to be friends but at the same time not wanting to get into trouble again. Fett just felt sorry for him and knew he needed to do a better job sticking up for him until Cooper could do it himself.

"It's ok everything turned out ok. We need to go." Fett tried to reassure Cooper to get him moving.

"If its ok why did everyone leave me?" Cooper asked Fett and he made a good point. They did, Fett had to think stupid and think fast.

"If the captain was going to leave you, why would he send me to come get you?" Maybe that would do it. It did. Cooper got to his feet and started to walk. Fett made sure he was behind Cooper so he could watch every move he made. He even told Cooper that he didn't need to rush because they had their own ship. Which Cooper then told Fett he was a pilot and he should fly them back to the No-Where.

      As for the rest of the away team they had made it back to the flight deck. They walked past Dan Fett's shuttle. Cheese made sure he was away back from everyone else. When everyone was out of sight which did take a little while because of the stupid amount of cloths the two idiots had on. Cheese slipped onto Fett's shuttle and put the device in place like he was ordered to. Now all he needed to do was call it in. This would be the ticket to get them out of going to the training exercise and then onto war. So, he hoped.

Chapter 12

Accidents Happen in Space

The away team was all back in the shuttle flying to the No-Where. The mood of the crew was happy. Jokes where being made. Mostly about the clothes Spu and Chris were wearing. The sheer number of items made it imposable for both of them to sit down. Still, they tried. Moose also tried to help them sit down. Maybe helping them sit down is the wrong way to say it but more fall over would be a better way of putting it. That was a Moose way of helping. Laughing at them trying to get up. Even Panda cracked a smile watching Spu roll around on the ground. Captain Cheese would normally say something to stop the crew nevertheless he just had so much on his mind. The crew would soon remember their fate about going to Fleets training exercise then the inevitability of going to war on the front line. Which normally meant a slow death. Maybe if the captain called the code in to the device on 1st Lieutenant Dan Fett's ship this would give him the out, he needed. He didn't have much time to think over his options. Soon office Fett's shuttle would be in space and every second he waited to make the call would bring the shuttle closer to the No-Where. That thought stopped him. He didn't trust Lord Admiral Miku or this Fett guy. So, what did that device do exactly? Cheese didn't know and had never heard of anything like this before. He pulled back on the idea about calling the code in. The better play was to have Arthune look at it. For all Cheese knew Arthune might have made the thing. He needed more time. Time to work out this Fleet crap and to work out the bigger picture of Lord Miku's hatred of Fett. Right now, he had pirates to find. Where did they go? Was he about to find them on the ship? He needed to know.

"Contact Gary." Cheese ordered Rush.

"Gary on coms." he answered.

"Gary, what happened to the pirate ships after they left the asteroid?" The captain asked his AI computer who would have access to this information with the scanners of the No-Where.

"Hehehehehehe." Was the only thing that came back on coms. The giggle was like a little kid laughing at getting in trouble.

"Are you high?" Cheese asked the AI computer. Which might seem a stupid question to ask a computer but somehow this AI had a reason it didn't take over the universe and kill everything. The reason was it was high 99% of the time. Gary the ships AI spent 2 years running every posable outcome of the universe. However, after pushing past the most common answer which seemed to be 42, he found the most fun way was not to care about anything and stay high. This did give him mood swings and outbursts of anger. The crew of the No-Where really didn't care about that because when it happened, they just didn't listen. It was easy for Gary to run the ship in this state of something that made him high. For an AI super computer it was nothing. He would be playing old games listening to music, running whole music festivals in programs that he built, all at the same time as being high. The simple tasks that would normally take a crew of 300 or more people to run the No-Where was easy. This did sometimes make it hard to get information out of Gary and this seemed like one of those times.

"Gary?" Cheese asked again hoping he was wrong.

"Gary!! That's me. I need a hit. I am hearing voices again."

"Fuck it" Cheese responded "Get me Arthune he might have a picture of what is going on."

"On it" Rush was fast to cut off Gary. It did take a little longer to get Arthune on comms. The shuttle was more than half way back to the No-Where.

"What do you want!" Arthune barked over comms. He liked life on the No-Where. He did what he wanted and everyone left him alone. Calls from anyone was an inconvenience to his day. The captain needed to be quick and to the point.

"We don't know if pirates got onboard when we were off the ship. Gary is no help. You got anything your end?" As this was something that could affect Arthune he didn't give the normal push back and just looked into it. This only happened when self-interest was more important than yelling sarcasm at the stupid people. Furthermore, Arthune was a complete coward and pirates on the ship is something he didn't want to deal with.

"How would they get in?" Was the first simple question Arthune asked his captain. Cheese did think this was an odd thing to ask nonetheless he needed Arthune help so he was just going to give him simple answers and to the point.

"They left the asteroid space base and would have flown in their shuttles and fighters"

"Please don't bother me with this." Arthune was back to being himself. This was only a good sign. He knew something the captain didn't.

"What's going on what did I miss?" Cheese asked with hope Arthune would fill him in and not just hang up the call.

"You do know that everything on this ship has a special tracking code. Nothing can fly in or out without it. You're the captain how do you not know this?" Arthune started to laugh "Wait if you are that stupid maybe the pirates are too, let me check" In the pause waiting for Arthune, Cheese looked over at Rush who gave the captain a look. It was a clear I knew that how didn't you.

"You didn't know, don't give me that look" Cheese told him as Arthune came back on laughing.

"Yep, looks like a ship did try and land. It was blown to little bits. Maybe two ships the parts are unclear. It couldn't be more than two. So, people are stupid all over the universe" With that he went quiet.

"I wonder what he is building now." Rush said out loud only meaning to think it.

"Big Mechs" Came back. Arthune hadn't gone yet and heard Rush's comment. If Gary was the AI that could destroy the universe Arthune would be the one that gave him the tools to do it. He was working on ships that could turn into mechs and fight on a planet as well as they did in space. Fleet did have something like a mech to fight on a planet but they stopped the program. They found there were better ways to clear a planet.

The captain was happy he didn't have to worry about pirates on the ship. It wasn't understood the number of ships the pirates had or the number that had been destroyed. Cheese didn't know if Shoe was still out there. There was a good chance he was alive, people like him don't die in a ships force field, he sent others to die first. The news Arthune was building Mechs could be a problem, he was thinking to himself. Was it more of a problem than having AI that could kill the universe or Panda's friend? At some point the whole of the universe was going to be hunting the No-Where after they did something stupid, Cheese could feel it in his bones. Maybe it was time to shut down all the problems before they got too big. As the captain was running the ideas over his head about what could be done the ship landed.

"We are here Sir." Rush told Cheese who looked spaced out in his own little world.

"O, Yes I can see that, let's get going" The captain said as he snaped out of his trance. He looked back down the shuttle seeing everyone's happy faces. He was about to change that.

"Remember we set off for war in 2 days." Before the captain finished speaking the mood had sunk. "I will be holding a meeting on the bridge in 15 mins to brain storm ideas to get out of this order. If you want to have input be on the bridge then." With this Cheese walked out past everyone on the shuttle. They were all quiet, stopped in mid action, the words seemed to do a brain reset to what was really going on. It would be unclear the number of people that would show. The captain's guess was not many, however telling everyone what was going to happen would stop the crew from using whatever the captain did against him. The walk to the bridge took 10 mins using the ships transport system. This would give Cheese 10 minutes of time to think to himself. Maybe he could come up with something.

He didn't come up with a single idea to get them out of the training exercise and then on to war. When Cheese sat in the captain's chair Spu and Chris where the first in. Mainly because this was their post. Still, they made good time getting to their quarters, taking off all the cloths they stole and getting back to the bridge. The captain didn't say a word, they both laughed and joked as they made their way to their posts. It was just a normal day for them. Next was Double H and Moose. Moose wasn't going to add anything to the plan. That's if they came up with a plan. He was there to do what Moose does. Hear the plan call it stupid then he could say, I told you so when it didn't work. He went right to it.

"Cheese I think we need to talk about Harry. Something is up" Cheese was not in the mood

"I get we should take him on away missions Moose, now is not the time" Cheese cut him off before the I told you so came from Moose.

"No that's not it." Moose tried to plead his case the captain was not having it.

"Not now Moose." The captain shut him down." We need to focus on the plan." Moose stopped folded his arms and was ready for the I told you so but instead asked.

"What's the plan Boss?" Moose asked

"I am not sure yet. I am thinking we need a reason or way to slip out of the exercise. It needs to be good they are going to know what we are up to and they are going to be looking for us to try something." The captain told everyone.

"No plan then." Moose was just trying to make the captain mad it was a side game he liked to play. Not just the captain, he did it with everyone.

"The plan is." In mid-sentence the captain stopped because the bridge door open. Was this more of the crew coming to brain storm ideas? No, it was first office Fett returning.

"What plan?" He asked. The captain remembered he hadn't told Fett anything about what was going on. He filled him in. Fett didn't say anything his face was white. This was going to stop all his plans.

"As I was saying the plan is to get out of the exercise." Again the captain was short and to the point.

"FUCK THAT." Fett shouted "that's not going to happen." Fett looked at the captain and said "you can thank me later." Fett walked over to Spu and push him away so he could use the panel. He moved the ship pointing it at the pirate asteroid base and yelled to Gary "Gary ramming speed!!" Gary yelled back

"RAMMING SPEED!" the engines of the battle cruiser hit full, plowing them right into the asteroid base. The whole ship shook with the force of the No-Where hitting the asteroid base. The base smashed into the ship like a wave hitting a rock. The water went everywhere, you couldn't tell it was a wave after the No-Where plowed over it. The ship took a hard hit. The damage would have to be fixed they were not going anywhere fast.

"Hull breach on deck something or other. You need to fix me before we can use jump speed." Gary told everyone on the bridge. Fett look back at Cheese and simply said.

"You're welcome" Then he walked off the bridge down towards his quarters. No one on the bridge said a word everyone was still in shock. Moose was the first to break the silence.

"I can't believe those pirates flew their base at us captain." Moose ended by laughing, it was funny it was that simple. Everyone was in complete shock Fett just did that. Spu was the next to speak up.

"Captain it looks like the flight path shows us trying to miss the base. This could be perfect."

"Get me Fleet Chris I have a plan." Cheese ordered with a bounce in his voice.

"Is it that the ships fucked." Moose asked.

"You two get off the bridge so I can do this" Cheese ordered both double H and Moose off the bridge. The last thing he wanted to happen was Moose making some joke that would give the game away to Fleet.

"I have Fleet Sir." Chris told the captain. "They have all ships data Sir." Fleet could check everything that happened with this data. Every shot fired, everything that hit the ship. It was smart of Chris to tell his captain that fleet already had this information so the captain didn't trip himself up. The view screen came on it was General Hamblin. He was a good General and came from a strong Military family.

"General Hamblin" Cheese spoke first "Have you received our data?" Of course, he knew this it was all for the show.

"Yes we have. It seems you have hull damage that will stop you using jump speed."

"Accidents happen in space Sir." Cheese replied.

"Indeed they do Captain. I have new orders for you." Cheese worked under General Hamblin years ago and knew him well enough to know he didn't work that fast. Cheese wanted to know more details with everything going on.

"So fast Sir? I would think it was going to take a couple of days to get the details worked out." He didn't want to say Hamblin was lazy in doing paper work because he was not. With the years of working in Fleet he was wise not to over work. He learnt long ago the orders could change 3 times in a day so you wait until the last minute to draft paper work so as not to waste time doing orders that would never be used. For him to have the new orders ready at the moment something happened was very odd and set alarms off in the Captain's mind. He was right to ask.

"I had the exercise dismiss order drawn up the second I saw the No-Where ordered to exercise. The only thing I need to change is the reason why you will not be going. I am somewhat worried that you only had 1 day left before you must report. Cheese are you losing your touch?" The General didn't hold back in showing he knew what was going on. Cheese played it off.

"I don't know what you mean Sir?" The captain asked with a smile on his face. Hamblin Smiled as he gave new orders to the No-Where.

"You have new orders sent to you now Captain Cheese. You are to report to the closest dock to repair your Hull."

"Sir, there is not a Fleet dock in this area we can get to." Spu told his captain. General Hamblin let out a little chuckle realizing he had been out played.

"What's the plan for a Fleet ship when it can't make a Fleet Dock for repair Sir?" Captain Cheese asked. This did seem a smarter plan than the General first gave credit.

"Normally you would go to a civilian port and be repaired." The General Answered.

"Is this a normal situation Sir?" The General could feel he was being pulled down a path Cheese had preplanned.

"This is a normal situation." General Hamblin answered. He could feel the hit over the head was coming.

"We can make a civilian port Sir to have the repairs done. I can only see one problem." There was the hook, it was now time to see if the General takes the bait.

"What problem do you see Captain?" General Hamblin asked in a telling voice knowing something was coming.

"What would we pay the civilians with?" Cheese asked the General. Now it was clear the last card was money. Captain Cheese was one step ahead.

"Ensign." The General said looking off screen at someone. The head nod from Hamblin was to check Fleet regulations. "Yes I am reading the regulations now. The funds will be sent to your ship with the crews pay after this call." But Cheese wasn't done.

"Sir, doesn't the regulations say for older ship's such as the No-Where extra credits are required to bridge the gap to the old technology." Captain Cheese did have a plan.

"You seem to be pushing your luck now, Captain." Hamblin was ok with everything to this point because it was following Fleet regulations. He was not going to give his old underling extra credits without a full check. He didn't need to check long. The ensign off screen had sent the relevant article to the General. The General read them under his breath.

"Bridge the gap to the old technology." Was mumbled "Seems you quoted the regulations word for word. The extra funds will be added. And Cheese, well played." Hamblin gave the captain a smile just before the end of the call. The General was proud of his once Ensign. Cheese just pulled a rabbit out of a hat this time. Not only did he get them out of going to war he got money to burn. Arthune would fix the ship for next to nothing, the rest would be for the crew. He had just the idea.

"Check we received payment from Fleet, Spu."

"We have Sir." Spu said with a smile on his face he looked more stupid than normal.

"Look for places to repair the ship, Chris. While I tell the crew what's going on."

"I have Sir." Chris said trying to be ahead of the game. "I found a moon 3 days away."

"No you haven't that's behind us." The captain said. Chris didn't understand the captains meaning. Nothing is behind you, when you are in space.

"Sir we are in space nothing can behind us?" Chris was totally lost.

"Look at about 7 days in front of where the ship is pointing." The captain ordered Chris." Let me tell the crew whats going on." Chris nodded and got to work. "Spu full ship comms please."

"You are on full ship, Sir" Spu responded

"Crew we have good news and bad news. First the bad news. The pirates somehow crashed their base into the ship and now we need the hull repaired. More bad news is we are going to miss the Fleets exercise so we can't make it to war." A loud scream came from Chris.

"A ZEDOOEN PLEASURE PLANET!"

"As you might have heard from the bridge, we will get some R and R as the ship is being fixed. We are not far from a dock at a Zedooen pleasure planet where you can spend the wages Fleet has just sent us." Stealing a line from Office Fett the captain finished with "Your welcome."

Chapter 13
Panda's Friend

The S.S. No-Where's crashing into an asteroid base got the crew out of the feared excise that would have sealed their fate going to war. Instead, they have ended up on a complete opposite side of a fight to the death in a war zone. They are going to be on a Zedooen pleasure planet for the next couple of weeks waiting for Arthune to fix the hull so they can make normal jump speed again. A Zedooen pleasure planet has everything you can think of doing. Humans mainly used the bars and casino's they didn't walk out into the alien areas. There was good reason for this. Humans had killed off or started a war with just about every known alien race in the known universe. Walking off from the main safe area where most of your race is, is not a good idea if you are human. Most of the crew would be in a bar. Some would be in the casino.

There was something about humans that wanted money. Money was meaningless in the scope of the universe yet humans still had not worked that out. Panda would defiantly be at the casino if his friend showed himself.

The captain had made sure that the crew was paid the back pay owed from fleet. It was normal for Fleet not to pay a ship's crew for long periods of time. The longer they didn't the more chance of the ship being destroyed became a factor. With the captain using Fleet regulations to get extra money to fix the hull he had a surprise for everyone when they got to the planet. The S.S. No-Where was sitting in orbit for a day and a half before the crew was ready to go planet side. This was nothing more than prep time. Only Gary, Arthune and Harry would be left on the ship. Everything needed to be set for the rest of the crew to be away for a couple of weeks. You don't need a drunk crew you can't find, that needs to come back and fix something that should have been planned for before they went walk about. Thankfully the crew had a couple of days in transit or the wait in orbit could have been much longer. The captain had the whole crew in a docking bay ready to get on a shuttle, just some last words before they boarded the shuttle.

"OK, settle down you lot." Captain Cheese said trying to calm the growing excitement of the crew down. The crew was very happy to get off the No-Where which the captain could see so he just talked over the noise. He wasn't going to get them to shut up.

"I will repeat myself when we land. We are only going to have one simple rule. Every day you must check in with someone from the crew. Did you all hear me?" There was too much noise going on for the captain to be sure. He said it again.

"You must check in with someone from the crew once a day! Starting today, everyone check in or you can't go!" The noise stopped, everyone started linking comms to get a check in on theirs. "As soon as you are, get on board." Moose was the first saying to Cheese as he walked past.

"O Captain My Captain." With Double H repeating Moose as he walked past. The rest walked in talking and making plans about what stupid thing they are going to do next. Rush was in the pilot's seat as fast as he could move. The ship was flying even faster. The trip down passed in the blink of an eye. Everyone was up ready to go but the captain was holding the door he had one last thing to say.

"OK you lot here is the deal. I got General Hamblin to give us twice the money we need to fix the hull. That means we have more money than you can spend here. I have made a deal with Rick anything you spend in his place will go on my tab and I will pay for it." The crew seemed too happy. Double H then asked.

"Panda is your mate coming?"

"Yes, he is waiting for me at the casino already." Panda didn't seem happy to tell the crew this, because he knows what happens next. Everyone from the crew gave him every penny they had to gamble with. He hated it when this happened.

"To Ricks place then until Panda comes back with the winnings!" Moose loudly pronounced. The crew even the captain walked down the ramp off to Rick's. Only Rush stood with Panda.

"Go on go with them." Panda told Rush knowing his friend wouldn't leave his side unless told. Panda walked off to the casino to meet his friend.

    Panda walked to the casino knowing his friend would be waiting for him. He didn't know what form he would be in so Panda was looking at everyone to see if he could spot him. This made a lot of people look at Panda very strangely. He didn't care. Getting closer to the front door of the casino Panda could see a lady leaning on the wall outside. This was a lady of beauty and class, clearly out of place, this was Panda's guy. He walked over to her.

"Give the body back." He told the lady. His friend 'borrowed' bodies as he put it from time to time. Panda did not approve of such tactics. People should not be a play thing.

"I like this body. People stop and talk to me all the time." The lady answered.

"If you want me to gamble for you, lose the body." Panda wasn't playing around. He lived by a moral code. Yes, he killed people. A lot of people, but they are all bad, God told him so. Taking peoples bodies is not ok.

"OK I will give the body back." The ladies voice said reluctantly. The lady then spoke again but this time looking very shocked.

"What are you looking at?" She asked in a panic "Where am I! What did you do to me?" Then with a slap around Panda's face she was gone. Then a voice came in Panda's head.

"You should have let me keep the body. You are starting to be no fun." The voice said. Panda answered out loud.

"Look God, I have told you if you want to hang out with me you have to act better to people. You can't just steal people's bodies." One of the many problems of being friends with God is talking to him made you look like a crazy person. If you talk with him in your head every now and then you would say the words meant for your head out loud. Not to mention if people heard you. Trying to tell them you are talking with God was always a mess. Half didn't believe you that God is real the other half really didn't believe and thought you were having some kind of break down. Crazy people talking to God in their minds is something to avoid in spaces with lots of people, like casinos. God did have one very big problem. He can't talk to everyone, only the clean of heart and people that truly believe in him. It's one of the reason's God tells Panda everyone he kills is a bad guy. It keeps his heart clean; he can help God with his second big problem, gambling. God has a very big problem with gambling. He was added on to the crew as a spirit guidance counselor so he could get wages to gamble with. Now if you are thinking 'but its god he can make his own money' that's not how God's mind works. God made rules for his gambling problem. If he just made the win happen what was the fun in that. If he had all the money, he wouldn't be losing anything. If he didn't have the feeling of loss the rush from gambling would not come. It was a great bad plan. God could only play with money he made. Which made it harder. God also only played card games to stop himself cheating. Anything with a ball landing on something a machine picking the number he just couldn't play. Sure, he might for a couple of goes but God is a very sore loser. So, inevitably he would cheat and give himself the win. This would stop the winning rush God needed, so over time he ruled all those games out, cards it was. Whatever the dealer gave him he would play. Panda was ok with the rules. He was very moral, more than God on some points. Something else that happened if God cheated at some other game of luck was other people would play. It was not a good look having everyone in the casino bet on the same numbers as the guy on the hot streak. It added attention which God or Panda didn't need. Panda liked to just sit down and do what God told him to do. The trick was not to act like someone was in his head talking. The casinos would sometimes think he was cheating and having comms with someone else. That talk never ended well trying to tell them it's

God as Panda doesn't lie. This time Panda had all the crew's money as they are well aware of what the deal with God was. They saw it as free money. Panda made his way inside to find a card table and settle in for a long night.

The rest of the crew were walking to Ricks place. Free drinks and free women all on the captain was something the crew was going to take advantage of. The captain didn't let women on the No-Where, this was a rule. The problems that ended up happening from it was not worth the trouble. The ship made problems for fun they didn't need added drama.

Moose was a veteran of pleasure planets. It was a good place to get bio-enhancements. Moose had contacted his good friend Mingo to meet him at Rick's place. Mingo was the guy. Everyone has that friend who can get anything you need, Mingo was that guy, on everything. Maybe Mingo would have something to calm down Divine Squadron they were getting out of hand just walking to have fun.

"I don't know where I am going to start!" Jig said to everyone.

"Doesn't matter where you start Jig, you will end up with me carrying your ass back to the shuttle like normal." Zig told him.

"That's true. Jig you can't hold your drink for shit." Alpha pointed out. "If you fuck up my couple of days, I am not going to be happy." Alpha gave Jig a look to show him he meant it. Cheese didn't care what was going on he was in his own little world.

"LOOK!" Moose shouted at the Cheese "Its Harry"

Moose was looking into the crowd off to the left where a man that looked just like Harry was.

"Harry is back on the ship" Cheese pointed out to Moose.

"No, look that's him." Moose was sure it was Harry down on the planet with them. Something was going on.

"It's not." Cheese told Moose one more time.

"I am going after him." Moose said to the crew as he walked off with double H following him. Moose didn't know if the captain was saying it was not Harry because he knows what's going on. Either way Moose was going to get to the bottom of it. The rest of the crew didn't even notice Moose walk off. Not even when the captain yelled.

"Remember to check in!" Moose didn't look back he just kept walking. Alpha was still talking and that's what most of the crew was focused on. Alpha was in fact talking so much the next thing most of the crew noticed was that they were all sitting in Ricks place drinking, all around the same table. Zig broke the spell.

"You can talk all you want but its never going to be called Alpha Squadron." Zig proclaimed.

"Is that what he is still talking about?" Rush asked turning to look at Alpha "No one cares. Its always going to be called Divine Squadron. I don't see why you want it named after you anyway? What if the new crew is crap and destroys the reputation of the Squad?" Rush pointed out.

"If that happens, we will change the name to crap Alpha Squad!" Zig said jokingly.

"To Crap Alpha Squad!" Jig held up a glass. Everyone followed.

"To Crap Alpha Squad!" Glasses raised people clinked their drinks. Alpha stopped his foolish pursuit of trying to change the name of the Squadron, for the time being. The atmosphere was one of fun. The crew was very relaxed without a care in the universe. This is the way it should be.

Panda was not feeling the same way. God was having a bad day on the tables. This again was normal. God would have good and bad runs. With the amount of money Panda had from the crew it didn't seem a problem to get back on top. Moose was hunting down a Harry that was walking in the back areas off the main street. The back lanes and alleys are not a bad area to be in. It's the area you would go to get things frowned upon by normal people so its hid one street back. Normal people don't walk back a couple of streets from the main area. Normal people just do what they are told. They stay in the Casino they booked, go to the best rated restaurants. That's Life. They are not looking for bio-enhancements, fight to the death blood battles, just a break from normal life. If you couldn't find what you are looking for in the streets you are in you just had to go back a couple alleys further back if it's not there then keep moving back, it's there. Moose was now in the back alleys following who he believed is Harry. He saw 'Harry' going into a place Moose was very familiar with. It was a place Moose had been many times before. The best Bio-enhancement shop on the planet. He walked in. The clerk knew Moose.

"Hey Moose" He said "We don't have anything new you are going to want. How is that arm working for you"

"Hey Eddy, arm is great better than I would think." Moose replied. "I was looking for."

"Harry?" The clerk said. "I was shocked that he stayed here and left the No-Where. That No-Where must be one hell of a run." The Clerk said pointing to the back office. Moose walked past the clerk heading to the office as Harry walked out the door with a hand full of papers.

"Harry." Double H called. Moose turned to look at Double H. His eyes sent a message of, you stupid idiot why did you yell now he can run from us. Which he did. Straight out the back door into a side alley. He couldn't out run Moose but that wasn't the point. Moose didn't want to run, but he did. As he was going through the door into the alley, he could hear Harry's voice yelling. He turned the comer and saw Harry on top of someone in the alley. He had run into them and both had hit the floor. Moose picked Harry up by his neck with one hand. It was helpful having Bio-implants people did what you want. The person Harry had run into was still on the ground.

"Cooper?" Moose said.

"Hi" Cooper said back.

"What are you doing here?" Moose asked

"I was helping you but I got lost." Cooper told Moose. Moose didn't care one bit about Cooper being here he was more interested on why did Harry run. He would soon have his answers.

"Why are you running." Moose asked Harry.

Harry looked at Moose not saying anything. Moose reminded Harry who he was.

"Ok I will make you talk." Moose reached out with is other hand and started to pull Harry's arm out of its socket. Moose didn't push hard before Harry started talking.

"Alright I will talk!" Harry yell at Moose. "Just stop, Moose." Harry knew full well Moose could pull his arms off without a problem. He had done a lot of work on Moose himself so he was well aware of what he was capable of.

"What is going on Harry, we left you on the ship but Eddy said you left the No-Where." The tone of Moose's voice was more out of concern. After all Moose trusted Harry to work on his body.

"I am not your Harry." Harry told Moose. Moose didn't answer him he just looked. Moose was trying to put everything together then he asked Harry.

"When did I get my last upgrade?" Harry answered

"The last time the No-Where was here about 3 years ago." Moose had worked it out, but was not going to use the WORD out loud. Just using the WORD could get the planet locked down. Moose then found an easy way to check if he was right. He pointed at Cooper and asked who is that?

"No idea." Harry said. "Someone I ran into?"

"If you don't know Cooper, you have not been on the ship. But you have been here. But you are Harry? That would make you a." Double H stopped as he too had worked it out. "A clone?" Moose looked at double H with the could you be a bigger idiot look which Double H quickly understood why he shouldn't use that WORD. If they scanned the planet, they would find the double DNA in seconds. The scan could be triggered by the over use of the WORD. It was one of many control devices set up to stop things that have destroyed the universe in the past and stop them from happening again. Clones were on that list.

"I didn't know that you can have Clones?" Cooper asked "Didn't clones destroy the universe?" Cooper asked everyone. Harry didn't know what to say. This guy was going to get the whole planet shut down. Moose and Double H forgot the levels of stupid Cooper brings and the problems that came with it.

"Who is this guy?" New Harry asked.

"Don't ask" Moose replied "Its best we talk back inside." This would help stop the tracking of words.

The tracking of words and other things that could get a planet in real trouble might be a myth. Everyone knows a guy that got a planet in lock down from a friend but no one had seen it firsthand. Was it something that Fleet put in everyone's minds just to do the right thing? Could Fleet really listen to everyone everywhere? Well yes very easily but they would need AI to track everything and everyone knew AI was banned and that to could get a planet shut down as well.

Inside the bio-enhancement shop new Harry seemed to be much calmer. He took Moose and the guys to a room that looked like New Harry's office.

"Are you going to kill me?" New Harry asked looking at Moose.

"If I wanted to do that you would be dead already." Moose pointed out. He had a good point. The second Moose found out Harry was a clone Moose should have pulled the trigger. Why didn't he?

"If you are not going to kill me what's the plan?" New Harry asked.

"We can't let you stay here." Moose said.

"Back to the No-Where." Double H said looking at Moose.

"Back to the No-Where." Moose said looking at double H.

"Back to the No-Where?" Cooper asked the room not knowing what was going on.

New Harry seemed to be ok with this. He told the guys it would take 2 days to move his stuff from the shop. The hard part was moving everything without looking like they are moving. It was a simple reason why Harry needed to go with them. If his old ship came into town and the captain did come and see him that would raise problems Harry didn't want to deal with. If it left without him on it there would be even more. He needed to go. Most of the stuff he was moving to the No-Where was Bio-enhancement equipment. Moose used the loading truck from the shuttle to speed things up. Cooper was surprisingly helpful in moving things he didn't seem to get tired. It wasn't all plain sailing with Cooper, it never was. The security scanner went off every time Cooper walked in the shop. Moose made jokes about it being a Stupid scanner. Cooper didn't get the jokes. Eddy on the front deck figured out what was going on. He to packed his stuff. The No-Where was going to have a new tec guy. Arthune would not be happy. After a long couple of days everything had been moved from the Bio-enhancement shop into the shuttle then up to the ship. They even let Cooper fly the shuttle a couple of times. It was the easiest way to shut him up. He wasn't that bad at it which shocked everyone. With the two new crew on the ship and everything on board Moose, Double H and Cooper headed to the bar Rick's place to meet the others.

    As they walked in to a very busy bar with people falling over themselves and girls everywhere, Jig was sitting on his own at the back right. He didn't look alive. The rest of the crew with the captain was sitting on a big table off to the back left laughing and clearly having a good time.

"What took you so long." Alpha yelled standing up with its arms open looking for a hug. Chris Rush Spu and Zig didn't move from the conversation they were having the Captain did turn around and look at Moose and asked.

"What have you been up to?" He was looking at his old friend Moose knowing if he had been gone for 2 days he was up to no good. Moose looked at the captain and said the words he had told him a number of times

"We need to talk about Harry!" Then Moose sat at the table to have a drink. Double H did the same. Cooper ran over to give Alpha a hug no one seemed surprised.

"Who's your friend?" Moose Asked Cheese about the girl sat next to him.

"Stripper." Fett said

"I AM NOT A STIPPER!" The lady yelled at Dan

"O. Sorry Lady of the night." Fett said. It was clear that her and Dan did not get on. Moose leaned around Cheese to look at Fett and asked.

"Does the Lady of the night have a name?" Moose asked Fett

"Captain's bunny." Fett said.

"My name is Crystal with a I." The lady of the night said to Moose. Fett was looking at Moose waiting to see what he said.

"Stripper." Moose said to Dan.

"See" Dan said to the lady of the night "You have a stripper name."

"I am not dealing with this." Crystal with an I said. She took the captains payment card that was on the table. Kissed the captain then told him I will be right back.

"Are you paying her?" Moose asked laughing at the same time.

"Where have you been." Fett ask Moose "I have been making fun of him, paying for Crystal. Alpha doesn't care so he was no fun." Fett said

"What, what's that about me?" Alpha asked

"Nothing" Fett replied and Alpha went back to talking with Cooper.

"Did Jig drink to much again?" Moose pointed out.

"Yea" Cheese told him as Crystal whispered something in the ear of the captain. He got up and moved away with her.

"So what have you been doing?" Dan asked the three of them. Double H was eating some of the food on the table so he couldn't answer he just looked at Fett. Cooper didn't hear him thank Panda's Friend before eating. He would just tell everyone everything in this crowded bar and all hell would brake loose. Moose gave him an answer without telling him anything which Fett picked up on.

"You still don't trust me then?" Fett asked Moose

"Not one bit." Moose replied.

"He doesn't trust anyone." Double H said with a mouth full of food. The captain walked back to the table.

"Get everyone back to the ship." Cheese said quietly "Bar trouble protocol Jig"

"O great" Alpha said tapping Zig on the shoulder "Jig protocol" They both moved over to Jig to carry him out of the bar.

"Is Jig being drunk the problem?" Dan asked? Double H moved chairs to sit next to Dan so he could whisper in his ear.

"No, we use Jig being drunk and carried out of the bar to get out of not paying the bill. Get ready to move." Dan looked at double and spoke

"Somethings wrong then." Moose just moved his eye brows up before saying. "Let's go." They quickly moved out the back got ahead of the captain and the crew carrying Jig. Spu then spoke up.

"Has anyone spoke to Panda?" No was the answer everyone seemed to give. Was this the worry? The crew had the money to pay so that's not the problem? Was it about the clone? They would need to speak to the captain to find out why they needed to use the Jig protocol.

Panda was at the shuttle waiting for them.

"I am sorry guys." Was the first words out of Panda's mouth. No one had time to ask him what he was sorry about because the next group came with the captain and they needed answers.

"Jig your sober?" Double H said seeing him running.

"Get on the ship!" Cheese said in full captains' mode with Crystal with an I holding his hand. Did he just steal a slave girl? Cooper was in the pilot's seat when everyone got on the shuttle. He ran past everyone and sat down right away. He seemed to have the shuttle ready to go.

"What are you doing" Fett asked him. Both double H and Moose said

"It's ok watch. Just let him be". Cheese couldn't be bothered with any of it.

"Why did you steal the Stripper? Fett asked the captain.

"Now is not the time to be talking but running. We can do all the talking we want when we are all free." Captain Cheese did make a good point.

"I am sorry." Panda said again.

"Free from what?" Dan ask's everyone on the shuttle. It looks like the whole crew is at a loss. Moose knows the captain knows about Harry's clone, that's why he never wanted to talk about it. It has to be that, but what is Panda going on about.

    Cooper flew the shuttle perfectly back to the No-Where. As they landed the captains first order was Battle stations. Moose was ordered to the bridge. It was about the clones that's the only thing he could think of. Office Fett wouldn't shut up asking about what's going on he clearly needs to be in the loop. The control issues needed to be addressed.

"We have incoming comms" Spu told the captain.

"On screen." Cheese ordered.

"It's just audio. It's from Ricks place." Spu responded

"You know what's going on Cheese I have no choice but to report your actions to Fleet. I am sorry old friend this is good bye." The transmission ended.

"What's going on?" Moose asked Cheese "Why is the stripper here?" Cheese looked at Moose he was scared. What had he done? Fett stuck his nose in again.

"Can someone tell me why we are running out on not paying a bar means they are calling Fleet?" Fett asked.

"It's not about a bar Tab." Chris pointed out it was way bigging than bar a tab.

"If it's not about a tab what's going on?" Fett asked again.

"We need to talk about Harry!" Moose told Cheese one more time.

"WE DON'T NEED TO TALK ABOUT HARRY." Cheese yelled at Moose. He had lost it at this point.

"Why can't you trust me!" Fett asked "I can help I am not a spy from Fleet you should know this." Fett did just want to help.

"Shut the Hell up Feet!" Cheese now started to yell at him. "You can't. Wait. Chris is the shuttle Feet flew back from the asteroid ready to fly?"

"Yes it can."

"Send it to rick's places now." As Cheese said that he held Crystal with I hand and said "I got this" A smile had come back to captain Cheese the anger had gone. "Is the shuttle flying Chris?"

"Yes. Why "Cheese cut him off for talking again.

"Can you move the No-Where away from the planet."

"We are sir." Spu answered everyone was on best behavior acting like a real ship's crew.

"Spu send this code to this number." Cheese handed a piece of paper. Spu read the number out loud

"TK427?"

"Yes, send that code to the number I gave you." The captain ordered. Spu sent the message. Just then the doors to the ship transportation opened and Panda stepped out.

"Captain I am sorry!" Panda cried

"We don't have time for that right now Panda." The captain barked back with his eyes fixed on the view screen. Watching to see if the code did anything. He didn't have to wait long.

Space itself looked like it was being pulled apart on three sides of the planet. The tears in space moved into large spinning voids of purple energy massing to a point. The points of energy in the center grow and grow until.... BANG! They fired and hit the planet. In a blink of an eye everything was gone. It was like a wurley death beam from space just killed a star. Everything and everyone gone. If the No-Where hadn't got far away it to would have been gone. The Lord Admiral wanted the No-Where gone. Cheese had an enemy inside Fleet. Getting rid of the No-Where would fix a lot of problems. The captain spoke

"Have you ever seen anything like that?" He asked Moose. Moose didn't want to tell him about Harry and the Clones. Was this the reason the planet was destroyed? He simply said.

"Nope".

"God help us." Cheese said out loud. A voice came out of Panda loud and booming.

"NOPE THIS IS NOT MUCH FOR ME I AM OUT."

Panda dropped to the ground as God left him. Getting back on his feet he said.

"I am sorry"

Printed in Great Britain
by Amazon